MIND HABITATIONS

...a delve into Poetry, Prose, Lyrics

By David D. Santana

Everlasting Feather Publishing Company,
Santa Monica, California

ISBN: **978-1-955535-01-4**

Publisher's Identification Number (Paper Format):
MH2023SANTANAMIND1968-PF

((Dear Reader And Fellow Artist!: Use The Pages To Draw And As Coloring Book Pages Creating Inspirational Images and Colors According To Inspirations Brought Forth By The Written Artwork! Appreciatively yours, David D. Santana))

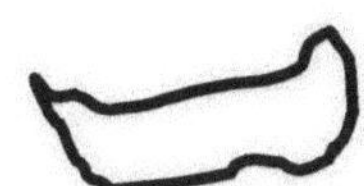

Dedication:

This Book Is Dedicated To My Mother, Rosie. Despite her imperfections, her intentions are good. She has worked hard ALL HER LIFE…slaving away just to make ends-meet! (…like most in this society). I forgive her for all her mistakes that negatively affected me. She was too young when I was conceived…not ready…but she managed the best she could. Thank you "Mom" for never giving up and for being an inspiration to me! And, an inspiration to the many people who have gotten to know the beautiful true nature of you!

This Book is also dedicated to **every single human being that resists** a society that does not serve humanity well. Those that stood up against tyrants and tyrannical institutions controlled by Corporations in so called "Democratic" societies and otherwise.

I thank you for **your courage and for your resistance.** Your examples have strengthened me to continue to pursue my eternal programming given to me by my Maker: God Father.

Father teaches us to RESIST the negative and deceitful worldly programmings so prevalent in every human culture and being.

Beautiful Father Reaches Out To ALL of Us! Seeking to bring us back home by way of **THE BRIDGE: The Palm Branch** Father has established that now stands firmly in His Throne: **Jesus Christ**.

I encourage you reader to consider many ways to help the whole (your community) rather than just you and your immediate family. That is, **to put on the Mind of Jesus Christ In Everything That Consumes You!** I encourage you as I encourage myself **each and every day** while in this world.

I also encourage you to have <u>daily conversations with Father in your mind</u> so that He may help you RESIST things that do not come from Him…and so that you discover what True Joy, Happiness, and Contentment is ALL ABOUT! God gave us a mind to think! Let's use it to evaluate everything and expose and discard all that conforms Not to Father.

If you get an opportunity, check out: **Eternoi.Com**. This is a grassroots organization that seeks to mitigate human suffering.

<u>**POETRY OF SANTANA:**</u>

<u>**PROSE OF DAVID DARSELI SANTANA:**</u>

LYRICS OF DAVID DARSELI SANTANA:

POETRY OF SANTANA:

Won't You

Written By David Darseli Santana

Won't you get around

And find a place

To Live Where You'll Be Fine?

Listen my love to the vibrations in your mind; those beautiful harmonies that **SHROUD** the linings of your mind.

My love! Those that i Speak to you about are the ones holding you through uncertainties that you and i are enmeshed **in this place**.

I use the "i" to indicate **this place**. Why do i awaken you here?

Why my love?

Because i love you. i love you!

There is no mistaken in what i say to you.

Because what i say is true.

From the deepest depths of my being i love you…you my reader…you!

i come to you and say "won't you?". Listen to yourself and listen! …take the time and **FREEZE** it! …and come with me on a journey home!

Won't you?

i know you can do it! i know you can. Come, let us be One again with D Thread…not stained…only pure…only love!

i

Silver Lights

Written by David Darseli Santana

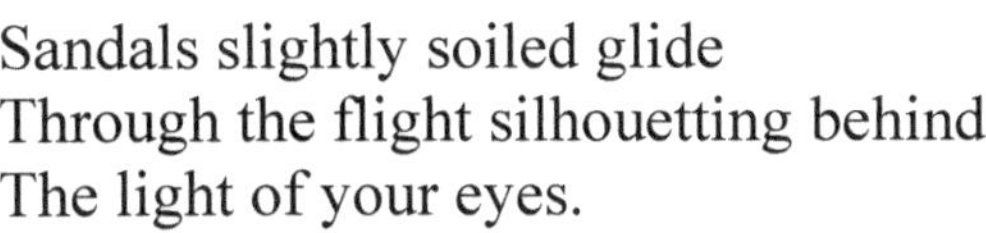

Silver lights glitter in my eyes.
Emotions bring back
Flashes of my being-seeing

Sandals slightly soiled glide
Through the flight silhouetting behind
The light of your eyes.

Such a strong sense of sorrow
Is sent away by the strong presence
Of your being-seeing.

Sa, Sa, Sa simmers away the

Seder state that streams through

My soul
Sedating it
By the light so strong which silhouettes
The sandals slightly soiled
By your eyes.

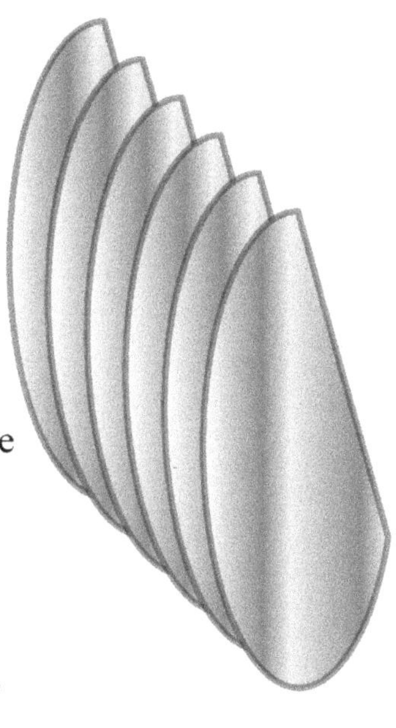

Silver Lights Blur
Silver Lights Glide
Silver Lights Be!

Glitter Be

Be Glitter My Love!

In
My
Eyes

As We Meet, Embrace, Sustain, Be

We BE BE!

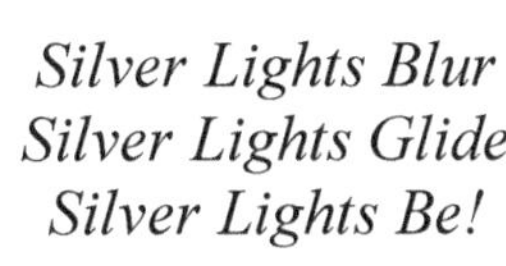

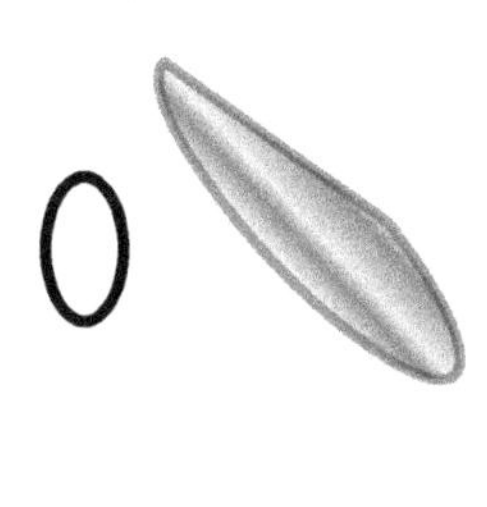

Be Work Key Be!

Written By David Darseli Santana

Be Signs Hope Be! B Faith Signs Be!

Me Be!

Be Shine!

Midst Be

Be Self Be!

Be Joy Be!

Be 'MMERSE Be

Key Be Key!

Key Work Key Be

Key

Key Be Key

Key MOLD Key Be!

Key Be Be Key!

Key REIGN Key Be!

Key Work Key Be!

Key Be Be Key!

Key Us

Key Be!

Key!

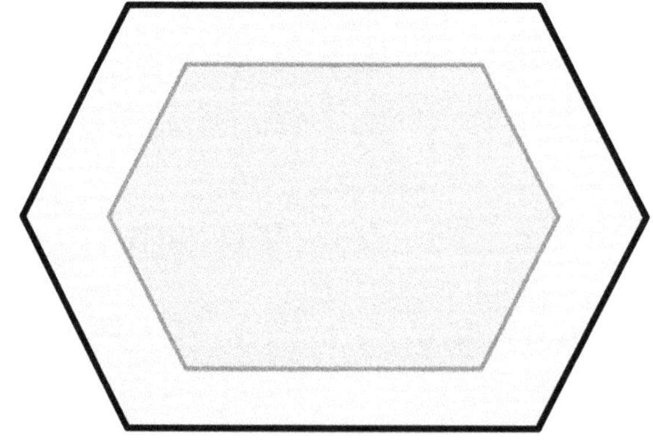

Spot Into Light-Light Into Spot

Written By David Darseli Santana

write in yellow?

skin a cat!

Glear Eyes Choose.

beings wonder here there

searching Destinies.

¡not allow doubts lead 'stray dentro confused state!

G-uidance Completes Faith Hope.

As a spot into light and as a light into spot

Hop Hop Hop Not!

Walk clear skies never dim never cease

As a spot into light and as a light into spot

Enter Through **GATES**!

A **WEDGE** Within You Holds **KEY**!

As a spot into light and as a light into spot

Behold I Wait At **GATES** For **YOU**!

MY CHILD My Love My Hope My Faith.

As a spot into light and as a light into spot

Walk with **ME** My Love!

Welcome! Welcome **HOME**!

We Are Now **ONE**!

Philosophy Of A Man?

Written By David Darseli Santana

As the morning rises
Clouds cover the earth.

The night still seems to cover us

In A

Glimmering Glamour way

What shall a man do if he cannot walk in the dark?

What light should this man seek?

As the man walks noisily through the streets

He recalls his night with his love

And

his

death

with

her!!!

What can a darkness bring? What
can black offer? As the man makes his way
up the hill he is actually going down!

How is this so?

Nervously the man continues his path

Hoping something obvious will appear

Nothing does.

It all remains

Dark

Gloomy

Unknown and lonely.

It all remains directionless.

*W*here will this man go?

What direction does he believe he is taking?

Is a man truly

In

Control

Of

His

Direction?

 I think not.

 The man continues
and abruptly stops when an iron piece of metal
At least he thinks it's metal by the sound of the crash
Painfully brings him to a h**o**lt.

What could this phenomenon be?

How is he supposed to interpret it?

As the man's pain slowly fades from his foot he decides to sit on the ground and think.

He contemplates all that has happened to him up to **this point**

Yet he finds no conclusions that satisfy his curiosity.

The man feels frustrated at coming to no conclusion.

He mentally fights his inadequacy

And

Then

Decides

To

Go

Forward.

Should this man continue or wait

For

A

Slight

Glimmer

Of

Light

To

Flare

Between

His

Eyes?

The man continues, motionless at times, through the path

The only path he knows.

Where will it lead him?

What significance

Does

His

Stubbornness

Have

On

His

Fate?!!!

Is there none?

As the man slowly continues his dark and non-visible path he hears other foot steps.

 He asks

"Who goes there?"

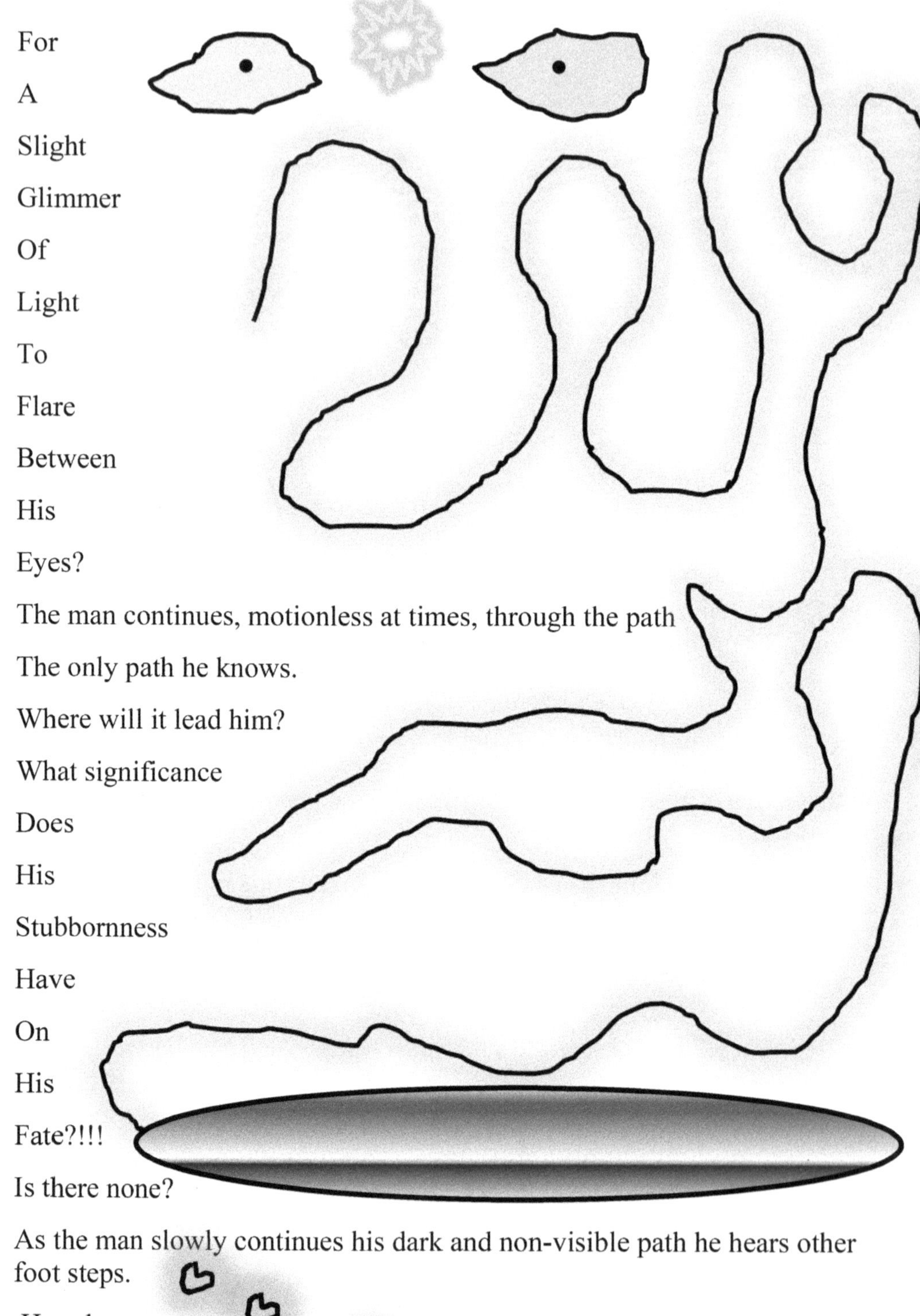

*N*o one answers.

The man is frightened

But has no intention on stopping.

 He simply asks

"Who goes there?!!" Once More,

And stops!!!???

[The Philosophy Of A Man is NOT ENOUGH!]

Tra - For - Ret

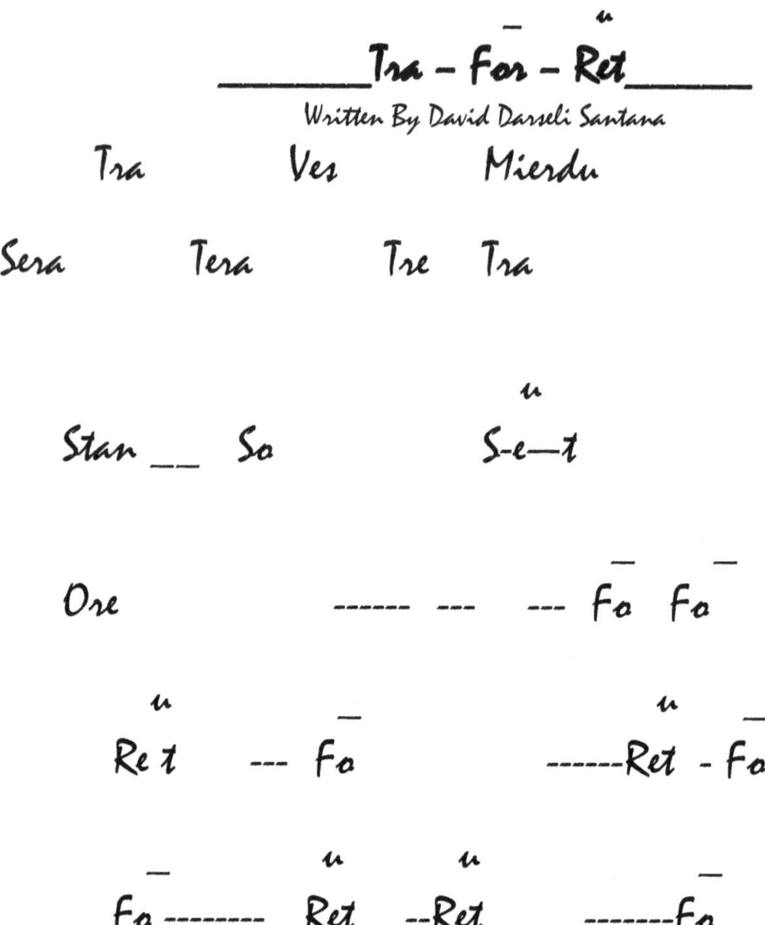

Translation: Return To The Right Side Of You Overpassing The Shit That Lingers In your Brain! By-Passing The Filter That Is The Brain And Way Up High You Will Find Your Mind Mingled Tringled Fingled Mindled In A Such A Way That You Begin To Understand One Thing AND One Thing ONLY: I have been with you always and we have always been. BEEN. How beautiful it is when you and I walk together away from the Rebellion Away From the Non-intended. I hold your hand!!! Go in peace and know nothing in all creation can harm you. NOTHING! For I AM the Power That Binds! The Power That is in YOU!

YOU!

MARK

Written By David Darseli Santana

Mark your calendar for the Touch

Touching down as I near the runway

Let's run a way!

See

Look above

What do you see?

Lock out

Is

A

Misfortune

Misfortunes are fortunes in virtues!!??

Various Winds Blow On The MARK!

MARK your calendar for the Touch

EASE Your Mind

To   The   Touch!

From Egypt To Jerusalem

Places of Coordinates

Connect The Points and There is your Mark!

There is your Home!
::
::G::
::
Be Not Afraid I AM With You Always!

T R A G E D Y

Written By David Darseli Santana

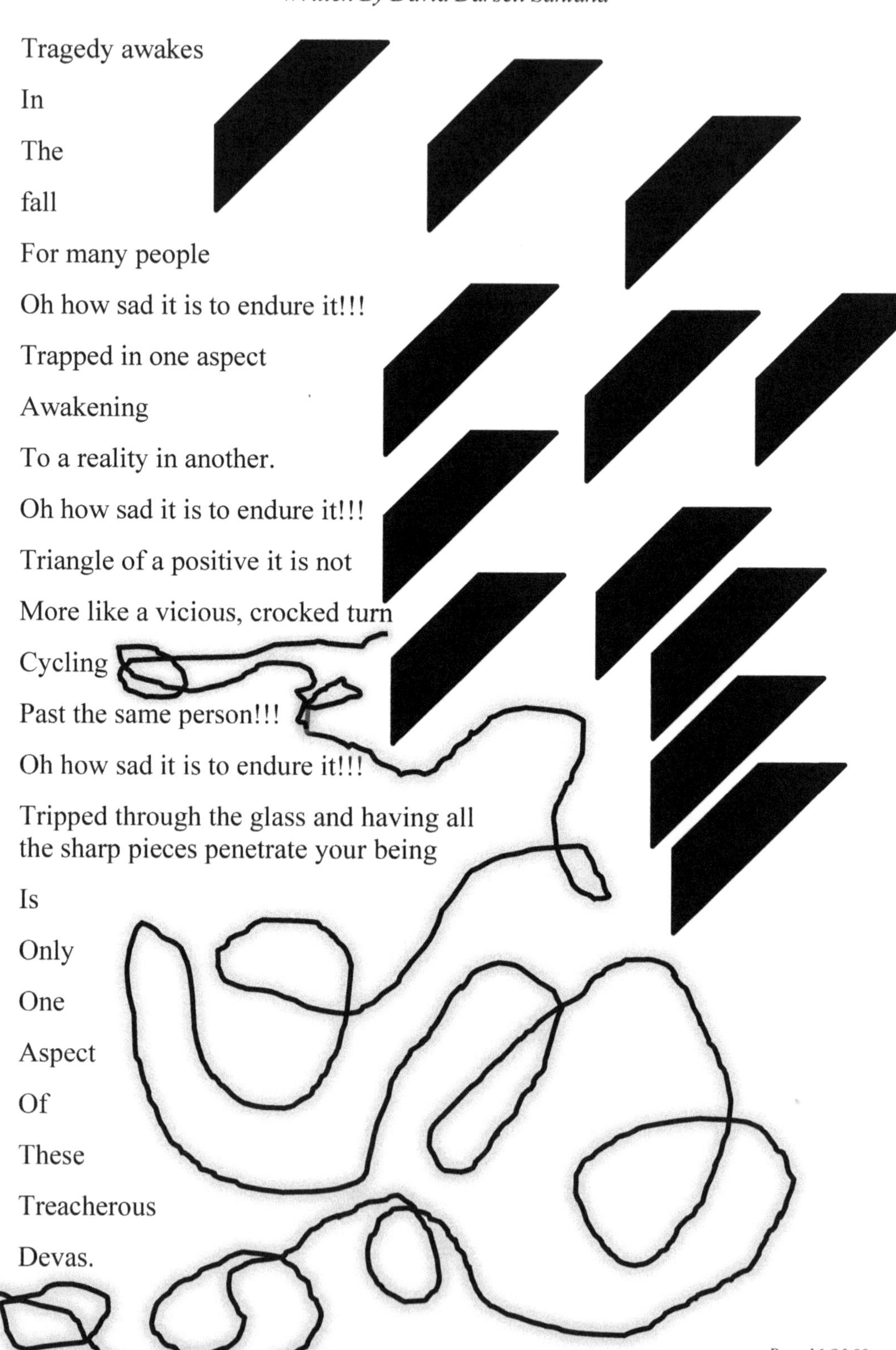

Tragedy awakes

In

The

fall

For many people

Oh how sad it is to endure it!!!

Trapped in one aspect

Awakening

To a reality in another.

Oh how sad it is to endure it!!!

Triangle of a positive it is not

More like a vicious, crocked turn

Cycling

Past the same person!!!

Oh how sad it is to endure it!!!

Tripped through the glass and having all
the sharp pieces penetrate your being

Is

Only

One

Aspect

Of

These

Treacherous

Devas.

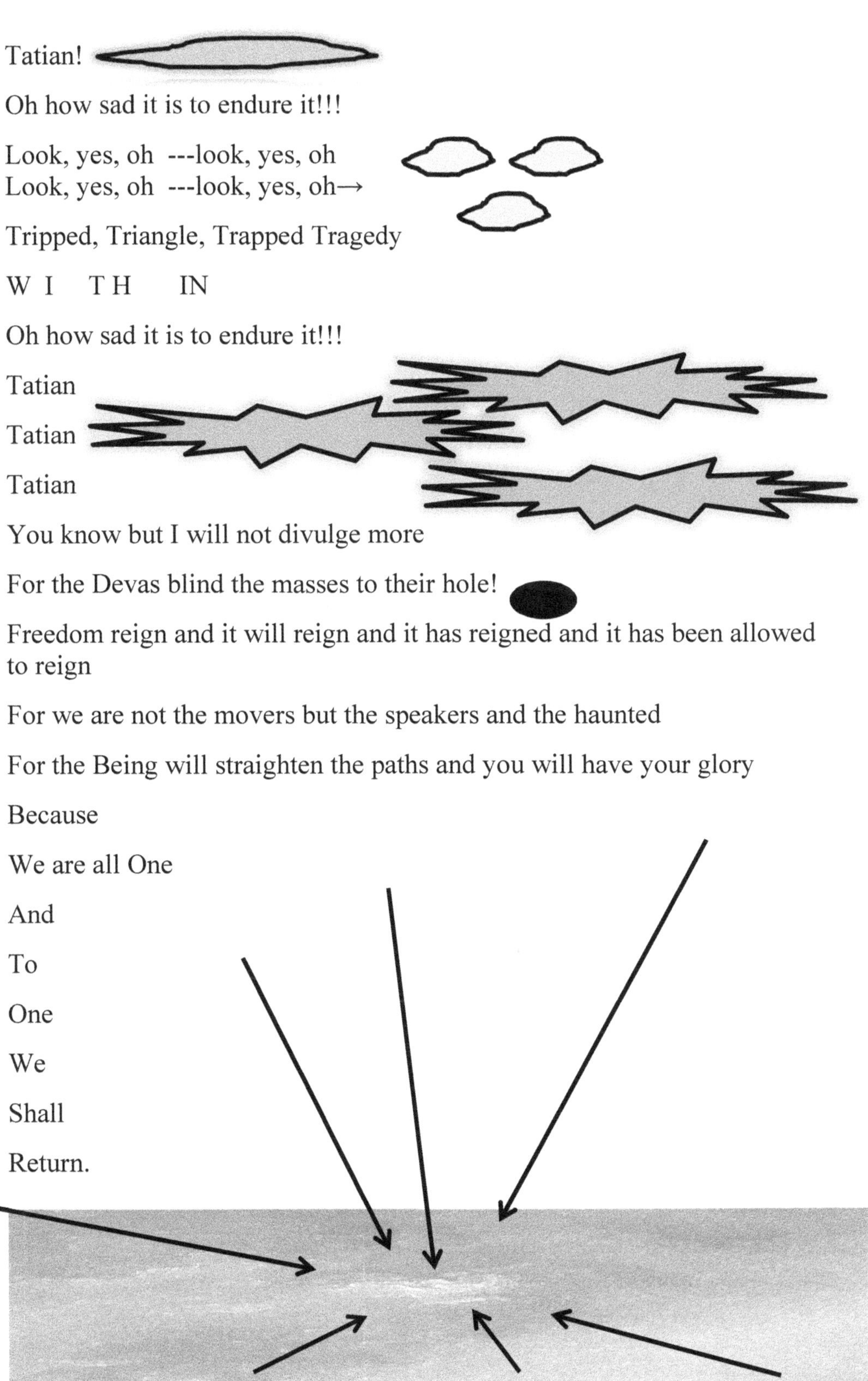

Tatian!

Oh how sad it is to endure it!!!

Look, yes, oh ---look, yes, oh
Look, yes, oh ---look, yes, oh→

Tripped, Triangle, Trapped Tragedy

W I   T H   IN

Oh how sad it is to endure it!!!

Tatian

Tatian

Tatian

You know but I will not divulge more

For the Devas blind the masses to their hole!

Freedom reign and it will reign and it has reigned and it has been allowed to reign

For we are not the movers but the speakers and the haunted

For the Being will straighten the paths and you will have your glory

Because

We are all One

And

To

One

We

Shall

Return.

Negros

escrito por David Darseli Santana

Buscando la noche
En
Tus
Ojos.

Allí Sé Que Brillas

Detrás de Las Estrellas

¡Allí!

Buscando la noche
en tus ojos.

Báñame
En
Tus
Negros.

Mírame en tu mente.

Buscando la noche
en tus ojos.

Buscando la noche en tus ojos; tus ojos.

Báñame
En
Tus
Negros.

Mírame en tu mente.

Tú dices que me amas.
Yo te lo creo.

Tú dices que me guías.
Yo te lo creo

¿Porque te lo creo? ¿Por qué?

Porque yo sé que eres puro yo sé que me amas yo lo sé porque nunca me has abandonado siempre has estado aquí conmigo así como con toda la humanidad.. y por eso te amo y por eso hago lo que me pides..porque en ti solo existe el amor la paz la alegría y, sobre todo:
tú.
el que lee estas letras que lo sepa por cierto que yo también te amo ¡a ti!
En tus negros estaré ¡contigo! ¡tigo! ¡tigo para siempre!

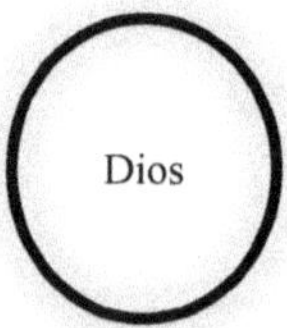

Hold The Weight!

Written By: David Darseli Santana

Look out into the Ocean
See the sea as it turns white
Smell the breeze. Hold the weight.

Rest your weight on the Blanket which holds marvels.

Rest your eyes on the Best View that cannot be
replicated.

Delicate views are but a perception
Let the Ocean precipitate you on to the Earth.
See the sea as it turns white.

Weather is not but one

Created by the immense of which
You see-in from within you. You see!

Yonder but don't wonder.   Trip trac
trow

Behold!

Look out into the Ocean.

See the sea as it turns white---white.

Smell the breeze. Hold the weight.

Hold the weight! ¡Detén el peso!

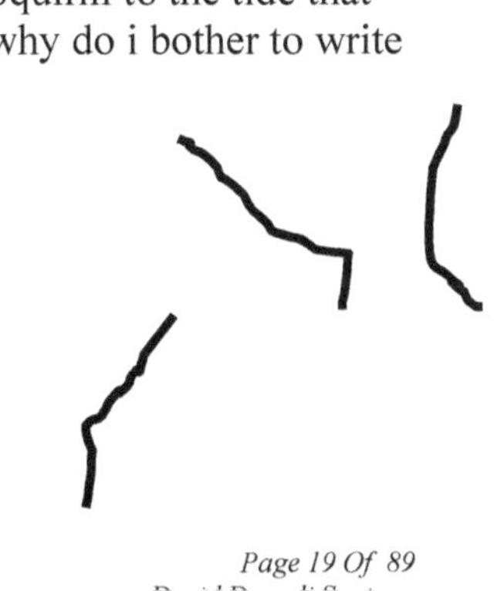

[do you reader u reader understand what i am saying to you? Squirm to the tide that
lies within u. search out that that is within you: that that..that why do i bother to write
some more for u? am i trying to help u? yes.. ..yes.. yes.]

[together we are strong.

and with the third we are Stronger: Yes!]

Grown Decay

Written By David Darseli Santana

The breeze was cold and dusty in the darkness
especially because
it was
in the desert
and
especially because
it was fall.

Everything that droops
From the trees
becomes
part
of
the
Grown Decay.

During one of these cold and dusty darkness nights of fall
A
Little
White
Thin
Snail
Named
Lassie
Began
her
round

Grown Decay

Grown Decay

Grown Decay

Lassie began her work!

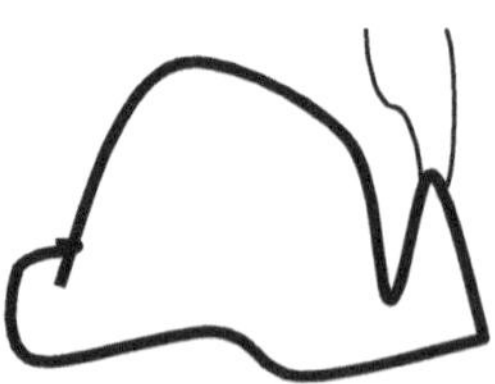

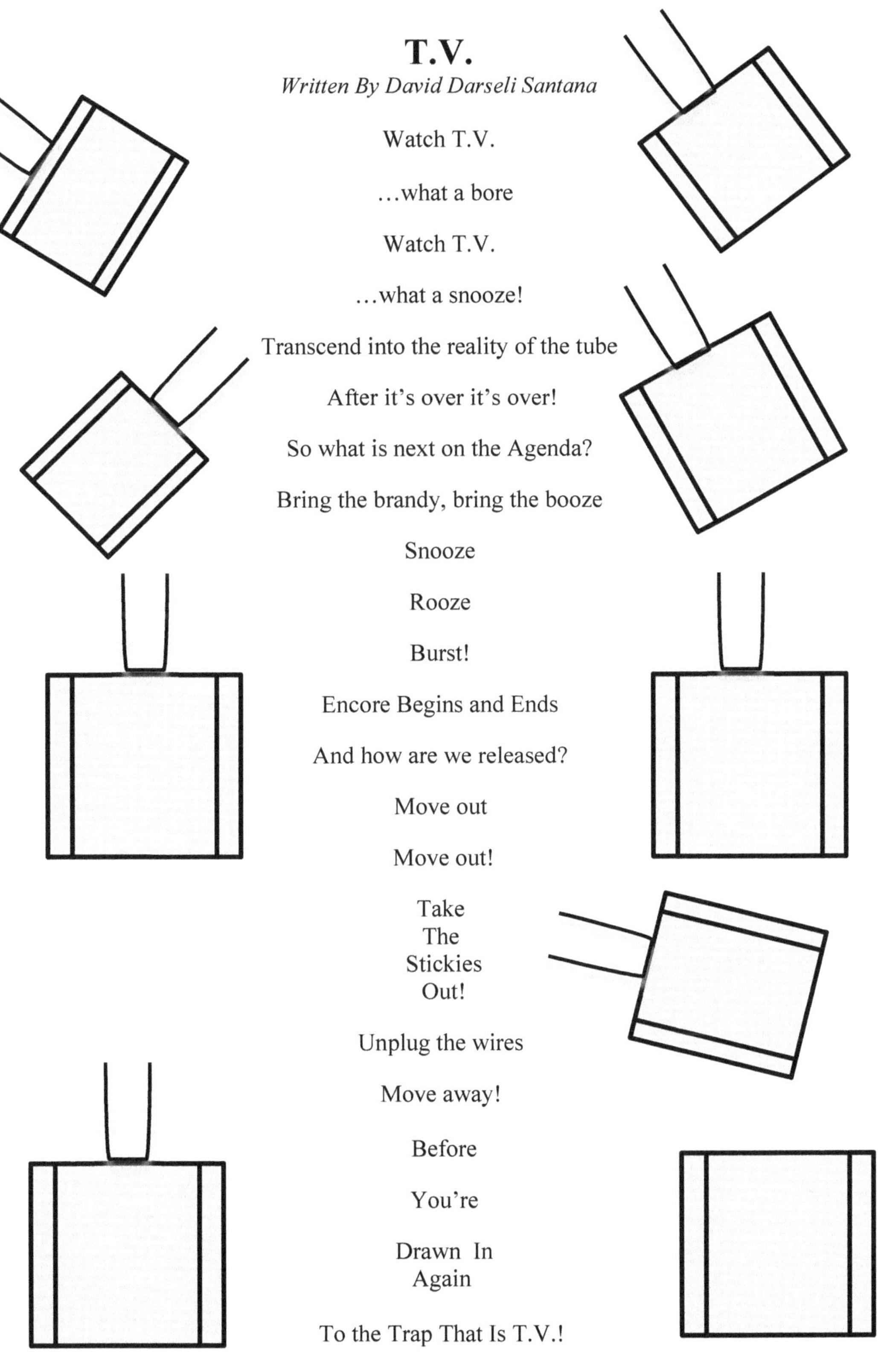

T.V.

Written By David Darseli Santana

Watch T.V.

…what a bore

Watch T.V.

…what a snooze!

Transcend into the reality of the tube

After it's over it's over!

So what is next on the Agenda?

Bring the brandy, bring the booze

Snooze

Rooze

Burst!

Encore Begins and Ends

And how are we released?

Move out

Move out!

Take
The
Stickies
Out!

Unplug the wires

Move away!

Before

You're

Drawn In
Again

To the Trap That Is T.V.!

Cigarette

Written by David Darseli Santana

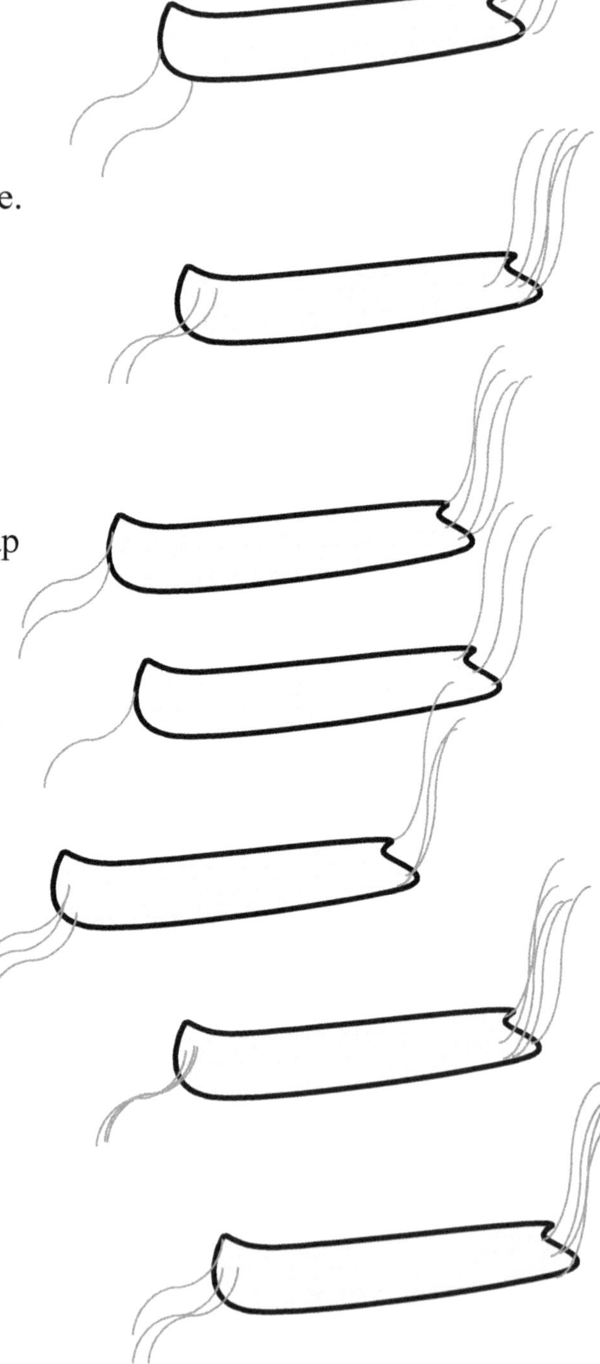

  Smoke a cigarette. Flare up.

Inhale fumes in thought.

Exhale and rejoice!

Smooth ride for a rough ride.

  Smoke a cigarette.

Fumes from teeth

Snaky fumes

Follow the trail… Gasp Trap

Inhale Exhale

Listen, despite bad wraps…

Although true…

The cigarette

Is

A

True

Companion.

In time of need…

In time of stress…

In time that needs passing

Smoke a cigarette.

Fumes from teeth

Flare up

In hale – Exhale

Follow the trail

Comoke
	Comoke
		Comoke
			Smoke!
				Loose ends cool ride!

一緒に向こう側へ旅しましょう、友よ！ 私
たちは共に、我が家という約 束の地へ辿り
着きましょう！

The Universe
Written By David Darseli Santana

The Universe

One Two Three

The Universe

All

Abstractions! Subtractions

Pulls and Pushes

Rights and Lefts

Transmits to Transfusions

Transfusions to Transmits

Brightness to Darkness to Grays Darkness to Brightness to Grays

Lifeless to Life Life to Lifeless

Fullness to Emptiness Emptiness to Fullness

 h a l fness, 3/4's ness , *bursts* and burn outs

Noise and Noiseless

Boom to Bam

Bam to Boom

Eternity Not Finite Yes

Boom Bam Bam Boom!

Fluttering Flutter Flowing Flow Highs Below Connections Flow

Spiral Influxution Defluxan Sealition Retract Detract…Gliding Home!

>>Home!

Grace Self

Written by David Darseli Santana

Spectacles of self

Self to the door!

Tie yourself

Hold yourself

Down to the truth…The truth Grace hold

You down Grace lead you to … Grace hold
You down Grace lead you to … Pureness
You down Grace lead you to …Righteousness

You Down Down You

Truth Open

Self Open Truth

Truth Open You!

You Open Grace

Grace Open you!

Night Wonders

Written By David Darseli Santana

Silently through Air in half.

The predators have found their day!

The victims have found their fate!

Loneliness becomes Trumpets fade

Night wonders silently through the air in half

Night wonders you wake
Night wonders you die
Night wonders you eat
Night wonders you play

Smell the halfness as it enters you Smell the halfness as it enters you

Smell the halfness as it enters you

Smell And Wonder Wonder Smell Smell And Wonder

Now My Friend Your Day Has Come!

Come Day Come!

Come!

And from the ashes I bring out what is to become yours.

Yours!

Melancholy

Written By: David Darseli Santana

Melancholy Down Turns Struggles On The Beautiful Life!

Sourness rains down on sadness squeezing it at it approaches

Overcoming the brightest of joys

Melancholy makes its moodmark moodmark moodmark

      Repelling it seeking to soar high skies high miles

Down tumbling the resistance

      Struggle is futile…time must run its course

Haste! Do not

Harshness! Do not

Tiny pebbles do not attempt to move!

Too heavy they are…too heavy for now!

Ride!

    Ride!

      Ride!

Wait! Wait! Wait!

Moments of Hope are on the Horizon---coming to you!
Moments of Faith strengthen you!

Remember and Learn…

      Melancholy is not a matter of mistime,

Ill-time, inopportune time

    unseasonable time.

It is the mistress of obscurity which clouds at any moment!

It is a mistress of its opposite while in this world!

Mistress of its Opposite while in this world!

It is not a variance but seeks to be an Exact.

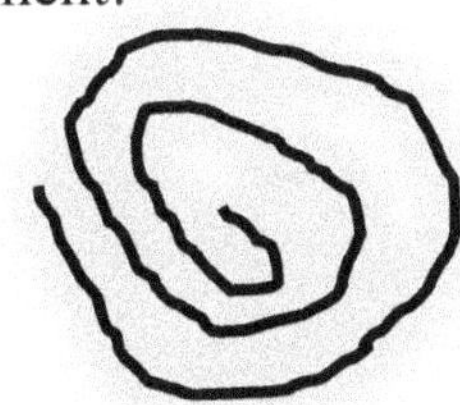

It visits from time to time to receive its dues as a tax collector does from time to time.

Beware!

Be aware!

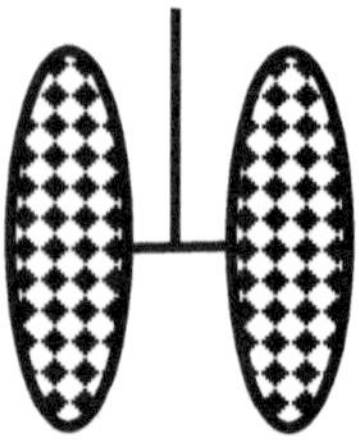

Haste! Do not

Harshness! Do not

Breathe…

Let it ride

Moments of Hope are on the Horizon---coming to you! Moments of Faith strengthen you!

Coming…

To…

You!

You!!!!!

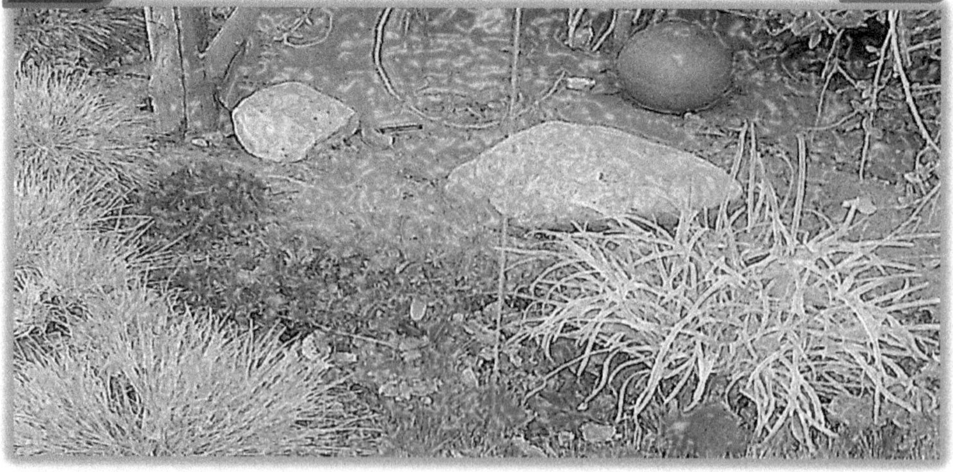

I Want To Show My Wings!

Written By: David Darseli Santana

I want to show my Wings!

I Long to show my Wings!

The sky is full of life!

And I want to be part of it. Show   Show   Show

The blue sky is calling!

The sky of colours Is calling!   Up!   Up!!   Up!!!

ARISE into the High Risen!   Up!   Up!!   Up!!!

And Away!

Away! Away! to the

endless sea of Life!

Arise!!!

Arise!!

Arise!

Away.   Away!

Away!!

Away!!!

→ Freedom, Duty, Salvation, Enslavement!!!

→ Freedom, Duty, Salvation, Enslavement!!!

Freedom..Salvation

Salvation…Freedom

Arise!

Arise!!

Arise!!!

UUUUuuuuuuuu I Long to show my Wings!

Wings! Wings! Wings!

up

go

i

¡Oye!

By: David Darseli Santana

Listen ! Listen my heareree My heareree.

Listen ! …   Do you hear ?   ¡Oyes!

¡Sí Oigo!

¿Oyes?

Oye, Listen, Oye   a   la   agua   correr en la

Arena. ¡Oye!

¿Para dónde va ¿ Where is it going?

¿Qué   vida   tocará ? ¿Cuál? ¿Dónde ?

Where?

Para ! Para ! Stop! Listen!   Listen!   Hear On.

¿Por dónde corre el agua?   ¿Por dónde?

¡Oye!

Sí , Sí claro que sí. Tú lo sabes. ¿Por dónde viene?

¿Para dónde va?

Where is it coming from? Where is it going?

Yes, Yes of course yes. You know it.

…. Where is it coming from?

Where is it going   ?

Don't interfere. Stop! ¡Alto! ¡Para!   Stop!

¡Oye!   Listen!   ¡Oye!

¿Por dónde corre el agua? ¿Por dónde?

¡ Oye !   Listen!

¡Oye !

Sí! Sí! … ¡ Oye ! …   Listen !

sí, sí, tú lo sabes .   ¿ Por   dónde viene ?

¿ Por   dónde viene ? ¿ Para dónde va ?

¡ Contéstame !

                viene por …..   Va a

sí, ahora   sí lo sabes.

                    Yes, now you know it.
              It comes from …

Viene   por …

Tú lo sabes.   ¡Contéstame!

¿Por dónde viene?   ¿Para dónde va ?

¡Oye!

¡Sí¡

¡Contestame¡

Ahora lo sabes.

Acuérdate. Acuérdate bien de lo que ya sabes.

Y

Sigue Oyendo .

Continue to listen .

Ya A llegado el tiempo.
Ya A llegado tú tiempo.

¡Oye! Listen ! ¡Oye !

Ya A llegado tu tiempo.

¡Contéstame¡

Ya A llegado tu tiempo

Oye, ¡Contéstame!, Oye, ¡Contéstame!, Oye.

¡Sí!

Y el sonido viene para ti…dando dando

¡Oye!

Things Hold Together

Written by David Darseli Santana

Things hold together
if
there
is…

a strong enough bond to sustain
the stress!

Although things come in many Forms…

the bandage material is the same! Strong! and Strong! and Strong! Oh how much

Is needed

when the stress surfaces the brim Of our understanding?!

Blue feathers move with the Wind as any other feather irrespective of its appearance and texture.

Texture! Is oh too often of importance.

Texture!

Blue feathers, Understanding, What the hell Am I Saying!!!?

Tex…Ture

Environmental programming we need to look beyond to find the true essence of who we are away from this prison!

Glide overhead in search of that precious commodity that only patience and devotion can deliver while in this prism.

Blossom forward your wings my friend and fly with me to where we came!

Texture blurs but i see you!

Come, take my wing and together we shall fly home! Father is waiting! J!

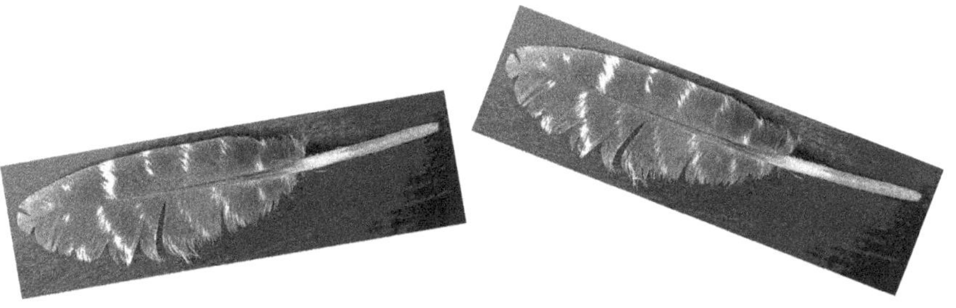

Two Innocent Virgins
Written by David Darseli Santana

An Inseparable Time…

If for only that moment

That space of time we solemnly prayed our souls.

Time in which space and time waited for us both. Two Innocent Virgins awaiting nothing but our present time. Time with Space

…shared a harmony which danced Our rhythm.

¡el ritmo del amor!

Oh you and ME came at our appointed time to combine our love and passions!

Despite the condition we were able to share Time for Sharing and Giving and Taking.

An innocent **Time**, An innocent **Space** [a laud to **T.S.** Eliot], which will live in Present for…Forever…for…Forevermore! **Vivi!**

Yes, Time and Space have renewed their wedding Vows once more!

All for the sake of existence...All for the Special Present of Our Present Time shared in love (amor).

An inseparable time and space.

An inseparable time and space.

An inseparable time and space.
Come Come My Love…for even though We Injured Eachother; We forgive Each Other's Imperfections in This World, In this Prison. We are Now Free My Love And We Glide To Beyond The Realms And Into The Sanctuary Where Moth and Rodent Are Forbidden! Two Innocent Virgins renewed we are!!! Sí mi amor Sí, And into Joy we Enter.

Enter!

Windows and Shadows

Written by David Darseli Santana

Windows and Shadows. Windows and Shadows.
Windows and Shadows. Windows and Shadows.

Yes   you see **now**!

Yes forward

And

.Backwards

That is

.sdrawkcaB

Windows and Shadows.

Into the depths of insanity and the depths of deception a realization unfolds

Inkquerings And Strokes And Elevations And Freefalls Angles Of Sorts

Points In Windows And Shadows Are Symmetrical Pushes And Pulls

Tear Down The Walls And Clean The Slate To Unravel That Which

Witch Befall! Windows and Shadows Spiral Down To The Point of Their

Inception. Witches and Wizards Lead Astray God's Good Purpose.

Heavy Hand Strokes The Final Blow and Out of the Wreckage You and I

Are Reborn **To Born No More!**

Follow the **B**, the **A**, the **C**, the **K**, the **W**, the A, the **R**, the **D**, the **S**!

…plain in site **Y** demurs the punishment and into fruition we go!!!

.sdrawkcaB

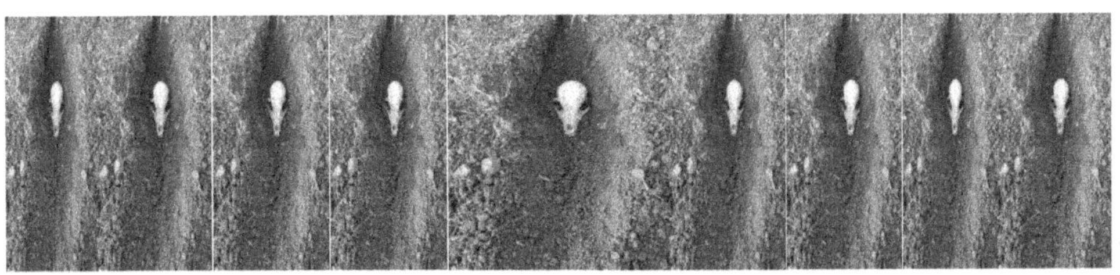

Morning Rise

By David Darseli Santana

The morning rise is ahead.

The bleakness of the dark surrenders to the power ahead.

And so you wake to another hope; to another chance at the troubles
ahead.
Streams of flowers wither with the heat of cowardness,
selfishness, greediness of the beast within us; of the animal inside us.

What! will become of us?

What fate will be our last step into the abyss?

Will you find peace?

Will you be in control of your being?

Who will you bow down to?

What will be our fate?

For now
The morning rise is ahead.

The bleakness of the dark surrenders to the power ahead.

And so you wake to another hope; to another chance at the troubles ahead.

Streams of flowers wither with the heat of cowardness,
selfishness, greediness of the beast within us; of the animal inside us

What will become of us? What will become of us?

What will become of us? What will become of us?

What will become of us as the streams of flowers

Wither with the heart of the falling fate That will not rise…Again!

Broken broken the skulls of man have come to an end. Hold still! Breathe!
Hold still! You! yes you! You! I have not forgotten you. You are on my
Mind Always. You. Grab My Hand and Follow Me! I wait at the door of
Joy to welcome you. You. You! Come my friend, come to Me, I welcome
you. You! you.   J   i   z   ɔ   s.

to another chance at the troubles ahead.
Take My Hand.

Silhouette

By David Darseli Santana

Gentle are the pours in your skin.

The inner quality in you outshines the outer.

But your exterior features mesmerize me.

Your eye brows slant to a smooth

Your eye lashes rivet with curiosity.

Your earlobes gently hold your beautiful golden hair.

Your lips although small show a promise to love.

Silhouette, I see the radiance inside you.

Silhouette, I see much more than just your lining.

Silhouetting, I draw you and then fill the features you expose.

The wonderful gift you received from *your* birth (*of existence into
this world*).

Silhouette, you are much more than an image created by The Light.

Bracelets adorn your smooth extremities.

Bracelets or no Bracelets, the slenderness of your skin caresses the patterns of
my face.

You ask me to compare your portrait of you…there is no comparing *to*
what I see in front of me.

Silhouetting you *with my* eyes and filling you with *all* the graces of
your skin.

…Gentle are the pours in your skin.

Silhouette
    Silhouette
        Silhouette
            Silhouette…
                Vibrance illuminates within me

As   I   Draw   You...

As

    I

       Draw

          You.

Silhouette

   Silhouette

     You   Draw   Me   To   You...

      You

        Draw

         Me

          To

           You

Silhouette

   Silhouette

     You

      mes

       mer

        ize

         me...

          You

        mes

       mer

      ize

     me...

     MesSilMerHouIzeEtte

       MesSilMerHouIzeEtte

        MesSilMerHouIzeEtte

*And here i stand at your door welcoming me into your crevices of **J**oy..traveling at beyond the speed of light onto you and inside you and all around you...traveling as i have learned to do to do from my prism to a soaring eagle of **P**ure energy.*

*Silhouette i draw you you to me and breath in you and with you understanding more and more where i am and where i am going and understanding that your essence is uniquely **Y**ours!*

Your holy touch is an extension of You! Y H W H...and there i find You! מידולא

Colgado En Un Alambre
(Ú.D.J.)

Escrito Por David Darseli Santana

Colgado en un alambre, sostenido en hombros doloridos. Soplando las
moscas que tanto buscan
En comer mi piel cansada.

Busco en quitarme de aquí. En balde mis intentos caen al suelo.

El sudor en mi cuerpo sangratea sangrando al suelo.

Colgado en un alambre, sostenido en hombros doloridos. Soplando las
moscas que tanto buscan
En comer mi piel cansada.

Sigo adelante con las esperanzas
Que la ropa sobre mi piel
Cubra y quite mi dolor.

¿Cuánto más aquí?

¿Cuánto más en esta posición?

Mareado, doy vueltas en el aire;
Sostenido por una desgracia.

¡Quítame! ¡Quítame de aquí!
¡Quitadme! ¡Quitadme de aquí!
¡Mis venas ya no aguantan más!
Mi alma busca aliviar su dolor;

Busca sacudirse de los rayos del sol
Quemando y atrayendo el dolor de la muerte
Ya al punto de llegar.

Colgado en un alambre, sostenido en hombros doloridos. Soplando las
moscas que tanto buscan
En comer mi cuerpo
Golpeando la sangre sobre el suelo del dolor.

¿Cuánto más aquí? ¿Cuánto más en esta posición?

Mareado, doy vueltas en el aire;
Sostenido por una desgracia.

¡Quítame! ¡Quítame de aquí!
¡Quitadme! ¡Quitadme de aquí!
¡Mis venas ya no aguantan más!

Mi alma busca aliviar su dolor;

Busca sacudirse de los rayos del sol
Quemando y atrayendo el dolor de la muerte
Ya al punto de llegar.

¡Líbrame! ¡Líbrame! al la eternidad.

¡Libérame! ¡Libérame! al la eternidad.

¡Súbeme! ¡Súbeme al alcance de la puerta de la eternidad;
En donde las almas encuentran su refugio de la tormenta angelical.

Dame tu promesa, Dame tu amor que lo que siento
En este momento

Se huirá;
Se desaparecerá
De las arterias
Que llevan un nuevo camino
En mi existencia.

¡Líbrame! ¡Líbrame! al la eternidad.

¡Libérame! ¡Libérame! al la eternidad.

Te lo pido…!te lo pido!

¡Libérame…Padre Mío!

Poet Poem

Written By David Darseli Santana

Oh I feel as though a sword has crossed my chest's skin.

It feels like a hundred hands have pushed me inward.

Oh inward! into the depths of me. Me!

Yes! Within this being who despite boldness, shivers like a coyote who has caught pneumonia.

Stop! Listen! Do you hear me?

Yes Me! ME! In this midst of terrifying loneliness.

in the Midst Of unfolding Known.

Dwellings I have known and indeed have been exposed to; yet; here I find myself being covered and cornered. …to where?

…In a procrastinating sense of Unfolding Known (UK). Wilma, Jake, Sally, Sam where are you?

I ask! Wilma, Jake, Sally, Sam----John, where are you?

Alone? … resistance seeks disturbance…a blurp…a fizz…a whoosh…a dagger

somersaulting into a spread inkquering a finger push…push!

Known pressure **pushing pushing**…driving **an obsession!**

…programming intervals cycling into designated moments

Boundaries are drawn.   - - - - - - - - - - -

Balance achieved *currents* Collide To Known!

Biting stings to prod the pen-hand me! Pen-Hand-HAND!

Le dilemme d'un poète. GO!!!

Water filled Nostrils creating pressure to the filter: the BRAIN!

…trapped mind beneath irregularities

Cracked Obsession Dies Dagger Mind Flies Nesting Secrets

SNFMDDOC

Le dilemme d'un poète.

Can I Write?

Written By David Darseli Santana

Can I write? Can I write?

Can I express the rest of-----Can I write?

Can I express the sense of----Can I write?

Can I express the press release----Can I write?

Can I express the depressed----Can I write?

Disheartened, Discouraged, Dispirited…

Dismouthed?!!!

I

Can

I ?

Write

I

Write

Write?!!!

B A I

Blinding Choir
Written By David Darseli Santana

Blue Skies Blue

Blue U

Flight Take Night

Right

Night

Sight Night

Nouvelle

Tower

Owl Outing

Blue Skies Blue Blue

Flight Night

right flight right sight right flight right sight right flight right sight

Is

Hard

To

Acquire

While

You

Are

Playing
Your
Choir…

Damn
That
Choir!

Ven Nouvelle Ven Nouvelle Ven Novouvelle

Radiance of a New

Written By David Darseli Santana

A Blossom in thy river

Sheds Radiance of a New

A New before not correctly conceived

Not clear because of one's own clouding

But now Sheds a Radiance which surpasses

All lights Of Known.

dark river flowed before

And flows still! In abundance

in n dark river

freedom is felt, doom is felt.

And all that shivers skin

dark river **meshing** darkness

And fable lightness

bringing subtleness

indistinguishable…confusion

deceitfulness…And this in shivering motion

To one's surprise!

Unpleasantly Uncontrollable Unconsciousable

Bringing forth an abyss that silently enters one's
mind…pain deceitfully felt

At conclusion

Of

dark

action

But now Behold!

A Blossom in thy river

Sheds a Radiance that surpasses

All lights Of Known.

Rivers flows Rivers flows Rivers flows

Which river attracts?

Which river **choose?** *NOT THESE!*

Remember

The river of Joy carries a Blossom that sheds Radiance of a New

---unpretentious and all forgiving---

River of Blossom

River of Joy

A Palm He Carries For You! You my friend!

Take My Hand!

In thy River I Begin To Bathe.
         In thy River I begin to Know!
  In Thy River I find refuge.
         In thy River is a "Radiance of a New"
that now I call home!

Come My Children.
      Come My Offspring!

Take Lamb Come Home!

"Radiance of A New"!

Ιησούς Nouveau Ιησούς Renouvelle
Ιησούς Renouvelle
Renouvelle
zuk
Nouveau

Vintage **P**erpétuelle

Written By David Darseli Santana

The Vintages of Time Amount To Memory.
Enduring Every Other Moment!
But Wait! Wait Oh Vintage For I Cannot Let Go!!!!
…of That! That Supples My B**eee**ing!!!!

A Being For You!!!!!!!

The Grandeur Making Of Something Magnificent I seek **not** to End!!!

End End **Knot***!!!!!!!*

It is *The Process* That I **Adore**!!! **D**oor! **D**oor! **D**oor!!

Between your eyes lie that which **Elongates The Essence of Us!!!!!!!**

Steer Steer Steer Mold Mold Mold*!!!!!!!*

Let's Keep My Love The Process of Excellent Making **Perpetual***!!!!!!!*

Let's Not My Love Savor That Of A Finished Product**.**

No no no!!!

Rather Rather My Love*!* Let's Savor The Process*!!!!!!*
Come My Love!!!!!! Take My Hand!
Let us be one!
…in the Making!!!!!!
In That Way My Love!
Let Us Be One!!!!!!

V i n t a g e **P** e r p é t u e l l e

the DATA
Written By David Darseli Santana

As the Universe Came to Be Through Energy
So is everything Within IT!

And from that instance…Life continues with no limit

Vicissitudes Flipped on Its Head Indeed!

A transformation…but the Energy Remains.

And within IT, lay the Data!

the DATA!
It is there My Love That You and I Lay In Welcome!

A Time That Cannot Be Altered: The Data!

We Can Once More Enter My Love That Realm That You And I
Carved Together!

the Data!
We Chose To Be One Moving Shaking Trembling Sweating
Holding!!!

the Data!
Come My Love Once More…let us Enter our Creation! Let Us Enter
Us!

the Data!
Our Blanket is That That Binds ALL. That That Separates ALL!

the Data
The Engineer is Here!

the Data
Nedged In The Numbers Are You And I My Love!

the Data
And from Birth To Birth We Continue My Love!

the Data
Father Thank You! Thank you Father for…

the Data

The 1970's
by David Darseli Santana

Naked people on the beach, walking as if clothed!

Rigid and Religious Politicians Seeking to Exercise Power!

Colorful Stripes and Growing Hair Dews!

Fuel Prices Reaching for the Stars!!!

2nd Hand Stores at Every Corner

Bell-Bottoms Galore!

Dressing for the Disco of Lights!!! a propagated distraction!

New Programming set in Music, Film, Television, Radio, Newsprint, Government, Business, Banks, And MORE!

…For The Minds of Children!!

Religious Peoples Preaching To Go Into The Mountains To Avoid A Pending DOOM!

And the SMELL of a T.V. Dinner!

It's All There FOLKS!

For The Taking!

[i wish i wish i hadn't.]

Again Maestro*!!!!!!!*
Written By David Darseli Santana

A Woman's Desire is *T*o Hold a Man That *W*ill Love her.

Such a Man that *W*ill Also Touch Her, Caressing her gently.

…Making her feeeeel *W*arm! Making her Come!

If she responds accordingly to
the Man (That Loves Her)

…Oh how good is that!?

VERY GOOD! VERY GOOD INDEED!

We take and We Give…veiled is our awareness always!

We Seek To Please To Love To Give: Reaching Over For A
Reciprocal!!!

…that entices Us To Be One! Reaching Over To A Reciprocal
…that breathes out Air Of Contentment.
…**MINGLING** trying to hold to an unending desire for
More!
Temporal We Seek To Extend While Before The Bodies Fall Into
Decay!

So Our Desires Remain In Motion!!!

Again Maestro*!!!!!!!*

 A Woman's Desire is *T*o Hold a Man That *W*ill Love her.

Such a Man that *W*ill Also Touch Her, Caressing her gently,
Making her feeeeel *W*arm! Making her Come!

Come Come MY Love I Am Here To Give You More While The
Night Still Shines On Our Ability To Give More! On Our Ability To
Keep The Flames of Desire To Burn Carbons Into Life!!!

Come Come My Love! I Am Here To Please You!

Come Come My Love We Are One!

A g a i n M a e s t r o *! ! ! ! ! ! !*

In the Eyes of Man
Written By David Darseli Santana

```
In the Eyes of Man
Shadows Swarm.
...attempting a connection.>,0.1
Linking Puzzles that are blurred. uuurrrrr
The Mind Resists!
...Accustomed to Its Cage.
The Mind RESETS!  Not Wanting To See Further!
```

"We Are Friends You and I" "Do Not Fear Me."
"Do not fear me!"

"Friend Or Foe?.....You know better!"

Silently Assailed by *Doubt*...Man is!!!
Most refuse to see **"the condition"**.

Waxing the movements.

Forging Bolts Around The Door **SHUT!!!**

Suckling Only onto the perception of the
CAGE!!!

Distracted by the **"SET"** Programming.

Awaken!

Exorcise-the-Body from Ur *True Self*!.....
And beneath all the *mildew*.....Is You.

You!

Reach And Grab That Cage! **Tear That Cage!!!!!!** The Cage Seeks Your Demise!
Transcend My Love And There AM I. And There ARE YOU! You My Love! Take My Hand! Follow The Palm Branch! He Will Lead You Out of The Cage! He Will Show You The Way! Break Break the Cage! **Your Power** My Love **Disarms** All The Components That Seek **Your Decay!**
And beneath all the *mildew*...Is You.

You!

And **Here** My Love, You Will Find The Refuge Your Mind Desires!
The Joy The Peace!

signed: **Father.**

The German Nun

Written By David Darseli Santana

Break Free!

Feel The Confines

Squirm Your Fingers At The Corners

Lightly Touch That Which You Have Forbidden!

Breathe Gently and Open Your Eyes.

Smell That Which You Have Refused! The Witch Seeks Your Demise!

The Signs That Control You By Way of the Alignment Of The Stars

Can be Broken*!!!!!!*

The Genetics of Black and White **Can Be Modified!**

The Zeros and The Ones Are **THE SAME!**

It is NOT about Deciphering…No No No!!!!!!!

Rather…**Awareness!**

German Nun…Go And *Transcend* the Physical Blues, Blacks, Reds, and Yellows You Frequently Place On The Pedestal You've Created As Your Standard!

Know that **THAT** Desire **is Not Ur Own!**

The Anger That Rages Inside You **Can Be Controlled.**

Control it!!!!!!!

It Begins With You Removing The Order of the Zeros and the Ones Placed As A Veil enticing your acceptance to Eat The Rubbish Fed To All Humans Daily Using Deceitful Colors and Sounds and Intoxications Of All Sorts! **S**orts **S**orts **S**orts!!!

Disarm The Dress: By Burnning And Spitting And Trashing ITT From You: The Tunic, The Belt, The Scapular, The Veil and **The Coif!**

Those **Red Mad Hatters** Are **Not From Me!** They seek your **repression** and to keep you at **despair of falsehoods**.

German Nun…take my Hand! I will lead you to True Pastures of Joy And Peace.

¡La victoria está en manos de la mente que te di!

La victoire est détenue par l'esprit que je t'ai donné !

Der Sieg wird durch den Geist gehalten, den ich dir gegeben habe!

unterzeichnet: Vater.

A day in thought at U.C.L.A. (The beginning)
Written By David Darseli Santana

A stupid feeling---I suppose!??

I feel like writing not because I am obligated to do so but because I am human.

I feel like expressing myself by all available resources that I have obtained from the human schools of thought I have gone to know.

It is safe to say that in this country, the United States of America, we are free (to a degree), I am free to write whatever the hell I wish to write about; to say whatever I damn well please within my capacity (and within the current order!).

Today I will write about life and my own personal experiences. First of all I bring you me, me now. I am sitting here on the third floor lounge of the Ackerman Union at U.C.L.A. I find myself dwelling in this place with other ambitious idiots, I mean people (This domineering world society has craftily created ambitions for us to follow…for not our end result best being, but that of the enemy! Yes, we are deceived…especially in the beginnings!)

Everyone here basically has a superiority complex problem even if they don't know it consciously. Do I have such a problem? I must have it since I am here among the chosen "cabrones".

I find this quarter system here at U.C.L.A. to be inadequate. Why? I find it inadequate because each session goes by too fast. Let me put it in a clearer light: you are required per course to comprehend very well in order to do well in about 10 weeks----a short time. You are expected to think deeply with interest within this time frame. And this is to be achieved while juggling 3 to5 courses at a time! Now, of course there are students who love this quick pace since they get it over quickly.

—however, such quickness does not do justice to what is trying to be achieved: learn deeply. I believe this isn't acceptable since the long-run-deep-thought of such a subject is short lived. Fuck the quarter system; let's make it a semester system. But noooooooooo, the university authorities want as many sessions fitted in a school year as possible. I suppose because they want the revenue; those fucking bastards, "hijos de su chingada madre". Oh well, can't cry over spilled milk I suppose!??? Join them or be swallowed up!

No. Let's resist and push and shove. Let's open our minds for a better world that puts humanity first…the human being before all this fucking technology! Take the technology and stick up your ass holes. That way both ends of the assholes compliment the other perfectly! ¡sí o no? ¡sí!

Oh come David, just give in! Yea is what they want to here. No is what we should do. Preserve humanity Preserve the waters and All the living things in them and around them.

Veganism and Vegetarianism! Yes! …everything else causes cancer and so so many illnesses. These cabrones knew this since the beginnings and have crafted society to be ruthless killers! No. Let's not go with the "yea" Friend. We need to resist! Let's Resist! For the sake of our children of the world…for all spirits trapped in these carbons! The Children Are Sacred. Sacred! J.

Ambición

Escrito por David Darseli Santana

Todo se seca en esta vida. El hambre se cuelga del pescuezo. La sed nos sigue hasta la muerte.

En esto entrar ¡la ambición!

La ambición no nos deja descansar.

Es un león que pisotea las éticas de lo bueno.

¡Ambición!

Es como un rayo rojo que liza la piel de lo bueno.

Sí es un demonio brotando hacia ti;

escarbándose en tus venas, dando la reversa hacia tu corazón;

hacia la base de tu alma;

robándote el corazón;

robándote lo bueno de *tu* ser creyente;

lo bueno de querer en verdad a tus amistades.

Ambición es un *orfanatorio*;

quitándote las esperanzas de querer y amar.

Ambición te pone en un rincón de la soledad.

Ambición no te complace; aun *cuando* esta sociedad te diga lo contrario.

Es muy triste verte en la oscuridad.

Te trato de sacar; aun buscas en someterme en las telarañas entrampazoras que llevas ¡'dentro de ti!

¡Te advierto!

¡Sal, Sal, Sal de la trampa de la *ambición egoísta!*

¡ ¡ ¡Sal, Sal, Sal!!!

Para tu paz y para la alegría acércate a una vida humilde como Cristo Jesus vivió cuando vino como Cordero de Nuestra Salvación…enviado por nuestro Amor que es único!: Padre Dios. Vente conmigo amigo. Vente conmigo amigo. Juntos llegaremos a nuestro descanso. Junto venceremos lo mal que es este mundo. Vente conmigo mi amigo…porque te amo a ti. Aunque sea imperfecto, nos perfectaremos en Cirsto Jesus: ¡Nuestro Cordero De Dios!

¡Deja las costumbres de este mundo!

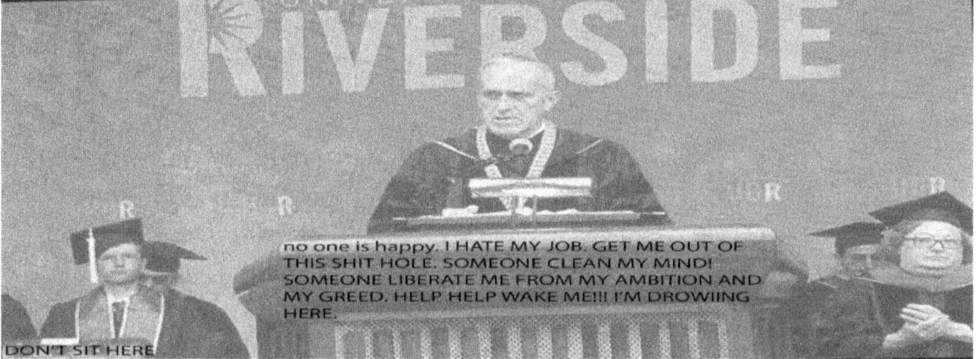

¡Deja las costumbres de este mundo!

Toma mi Mano

Abre La Mente

Toma mi Mano

Abre La Mente

Y allí mi amor estaré Yo para Ti Siempre

Toma mi Mano

Estrada

Escrito Por David Darseli Santana

Estrada caminaba por la pradera de su hogar.

En un desfile de flores----rojas, verdes, amarillas, y anaranjadas, vio una bella de piel y sangre, con ojos azules y boca roja, cejas gruesas y negras, ancha y chata su nariz.

Ella fue hecha con el amor prohibido en los tiempos antiguos.

Estrada la vio, asombrado y agarrado de la tranza, inmovilizado, asustado. Vio sus trenzas deslizarse al viento y fue alborotado por la belleza en la pradera.

La impurezió con su tentación: la agarró y la sentó; abrió sus alas y la sometió a la eternidad: donde el mar junta los solos para formar una criatura que brotará hacia la vida.

     Llegó el momento para dar tiempo a conocer a la criatura y darle
amor.

Estrada negó la tentación que dio hace un año; se encabronó y dejó la bella llorando, y sin esperanzas para el bebé.

Se casó Estrada en la pradera donde hizo su tentación.

La otra mujer recién casada con Estrada ¡se enceló con el niño
abandonado!

"¿Qué culpa tiene la criatura de los hechos de este sinvergüenza que poco hombre no llegó?"

Estrada, Estrada ¡recupera tu valor!

¡Recupera!

Boom **Bam**

Written By: David Darseli Santana

My head is bursting. The spiders are crawling from my head. I try to keep them from forming yet the social turmoil in my life is slowly creeping and sliding cracks in my skull. My eyes are seeing less and less. My focus is dissipating and is waiting in a gloss that's getting whiter.

My lips are open, my mouth is open. There's no movement---no expression for the lesion that prizes itself in destroying the born. My ears are numb that not even drums can shake-wake. intentional evil incision is carving me onto antimatter!

I'm losing my senses and fading away. I cannot take it anymore. I am I am
I am
..........GOING INSANE!!!
No one sees me, no one helps me. Everyone judges, points the finger and doesn't help!

I am GOING INSANE!!! I'm losing my mind. I try so hard to keep alive, to do what's right yet everyone is against me. Oh if you would know everything you would understand. Oh if you would know everything you would understand.

I am GOING INSANE!!! No one to stop me. I'm going forward and never returning. Is this good for society? I don't know but here I come. I wish I could stay and be part of life. Tears are drying, my skull is sealing with the elements to destroy, to destroy, to destroy and to be destroyed.

No more fear, no more doubts, I going to destroy this world with my new face; a face I didn't choose a face that was pushed onto me by the Cancer-Spreading Capitalist Eating Societies, by the egotistic population, by the selfish minds that cannot find the elements of true love, the elements of true giving.

I am GOING INSANE!!!

"Oh God, I'm sorry. This is the way I must learn for no other way opened my eyes, my ears, my mouth for a better, truly better tomorrow"

Boom   Bam! ... dead i am!...

dead, you're all dead!!!

but wait!!! wait!! Wait!
…..   ……………..   ………….   ………   ……..
i listened to your plea…u held me still…**wait!**...you said. i listened to u and shun away

the evil that sought to overcome me by ruthless impulses of a material world!

…God saved me right before i let loose my insanity. God kept me. Thank you God for opening my eyes!…for allowing me to see me without the lights and the glares and the

fuzz and the sell! down down *tubling* <u>down</u> i **rise** with a new hope and a new faith tillith my Maker save me from this place of sullen faces pressed by the heartless back seaters. save i am. It is through true community that we save one another from dwelling evil inside inside inside this contaminated Carbon!!!...not from God from evil…Hand i reach! Hand Savith me! me! me! And to your Kingdom i delve…Salvation savith me! Hand J!

Standing On A Fragile Platform

Written By: David Darseli Santana

Deem me incompetent for the world is the judge or should I say the powers that be?

Which way will you rule? Am I good or bad? Which way will you sway, up or down?

Rising to the occasion I present myself to you. Standing on a fragile platform, I dare not look at you. Oh mister power, oh misses power, how will you judge me? Should I live or die?

Yes sir maam, I was born in 1968 on the height of our rebellion. We sought not much, just freedom from your shit! You asshole! You bitch! You puta! You maricon! Which way will you sway?

Now it is true, we did try. We did stand. We did speak out. But wait! We did not beat you. We did not shoot you. We simply spoke: Get off our backs! Get off our backs! Don't set us loose again into your shit! We don't want to be fed.

We want to be free, free!

Just in time I come to you before you cut my balls off; before you string me up on that tree, before you pull the cord and let me die; before you kill me by the blade of your sword. You fuck; you son of a bitch! Wait here! I've got something for you! Dwell on this; wear this. How does it feel? Does it fit, you bitch, you punk without funk!

We say no, ¡No más! We say, watch your back, you might slip; you might fall. Fall!, Fall!---I'll pull you down I'll set you down. Fall!, Fall!

No more straws but our fists! No more massage but our teeth!

No more! No more! No more!

You're going down!

You're going down!

Y o u ' re …g o ing… d o wn!!!!

Viva la Revolución Galaxie

El Amor a la Música

Written By: David Darseli Santana

No quiero ser nada menos tocar y oír mi música.

Estoy aquí en el trabajo pero mi mente está en las frases que he escrito, con la melodía que he formado, y en el interés que está por nacer.

No quiero hacer nada más que tocar y oír mí música e escribir nuevos versos, tonos en mi guitarra.

Las problemas quieren apoderarse de mi tiempo----pero no, no, no; no voy a tomar el tiempo en escucharlas y estar en la negatividad.

Lo más que me meto en mi música lo menos quiero de esta vida---- sólo quiero amor y compasión, sólo quiero el amor que tú me das, las inspiraciones del baile, e escribir las melodías esperando a nacer.

Explosión de alegría yo siento cuando oigo sonidos como éstos que he escrito: "Montaña rusa, estoy montado con la fuerza de un cañón; nada me quita, nada me tumba."

¡El amor a la música es el amor que tengo para ti!

¡Pero, el amor a la música es primordial en mi ser; en mi mente!

El amor a la música.

El amor a la música.

El amor a la música.

Vente Conmigo A La Continuación de la Eternidad!

Muñeca
Escucha Mi Requête

Written By: David Darseli Santana

Me pongo a *frissoner* al instante que te veo cayendo a la oscuridad. La muerte te persigue cada vez que tu *plonger* a la camilla que tu vendes.

Muñeca mía escucha mi *requête.* Sal de esa *damnation.* No seas un *salope.*

Tard viene la noche. *Teigne* y más es el peligro. También la *démoralisation* de tu vida te pone en peligro; Quita esa *démoralisation* de tu dignidad.

Muñeca mía escucha mi *requête.* Sal de esa *damnation.* No seas un *salope.*

Monstre te me estás poniendo. La inocencia se te está muriendo. En *montant* grande te vas cayendo. *Ployer* va tu corazón.

Muñeca mía escucha mi *requête.* Sal de esa *damnation.* No seas un *salope.*

La Muert------e viene rápido.

Nace mi amor a la luz del Padre Celestial que estira su Mano para recibirte.

Ven mi amor…Ven conmigo a nuestro origen. Ven mi amore.

¡Ven!

The Imperfect Wise Man
(In Time)
Written By David Darseli Santana

Your eyes are old, they've seen so much.

You've got wisdom that patiently accepts what *we* are.

The wrinkles in your face are like the rings in a tree.

They've seen so much… and have aged in this mechanism we call time.

You've seen so much light in your life; you've opened your eyes, you've seen the Light.

And although at times you've rejected this Light, time has given you time to realize, to learn, and to accept the Wisdom of God.

The white hair on your head proves that you've lived in time for a long time; in hope for a long time; and in darkness for a long time---and yet this time shines on like a spot on the moon that lights up the sky.

Your eyes are old, they've seen so much.

You've got wisdom that patiently accepts what *you* are.

The winkles in your face are like the rings in a tree.

They've seen so much… and have aged in this mechanism we call time.

The spots on your head
Are like the spots on the sun…
…they've been on a being that lived so long

A being that brings wisdom and life to the young, to the meek, to the children who proceed this dying bright---which nourishes the next.

…so that they can too one day be that beacon of Bright.

And although at times you've rejected this Light, time has given you time to realize, to learn, and to accept the wisdom of God Father.

> The spots on your head
> Are like the spots on the sun…
> …they've been on a being that lived so long
>
> A being that brings wisdom and life to the young, to the meek, to the children who proceed this dying bright--- which nourishes the next...
> …so that they can too one day be that beacon of Bright.
>
> The beacon of bright that still shines on you……to that new place you have gone to!
>
> God speed EMK!

Love Established

Written By David Darseli Santana

Once

Love

Is

ESTABLISHED…

It

Is

F O R E V E R!

What More Can A Man Want When A Guarantee Is Placed In Blood?

How Else Are We To Interpret A Sacrifice Willingly For The Sake Of Love?

Fear Deteriorates For It Has No Real Power Over Love.

Of all the Doubts, None Will Survive The Coming Love That Has Come!

For In the Blood We Know That In Our Current Prison We Will Not Be Held!

Because…

Once

Love

Is

ESTABLISHED…

It

Is

F O R E V E R!

My Yellow Rose
Written By David Darseli Santana

A yellow rose comes shivering down

After it has been pushed by the wind.

It's soft skin embraces the soil beneath

and

finds refuge from the forces above.

It lies motionless…thinking if it will ever rise.

Rise to see its companions who will no doubt find themselves in the same fate as the fallen One.

But behold!

This fallen creature will be lifted again by the very same wind which brought it to its fate.

This wind will be its Salvation and will give it Haven…

if only

to be transported to another place.

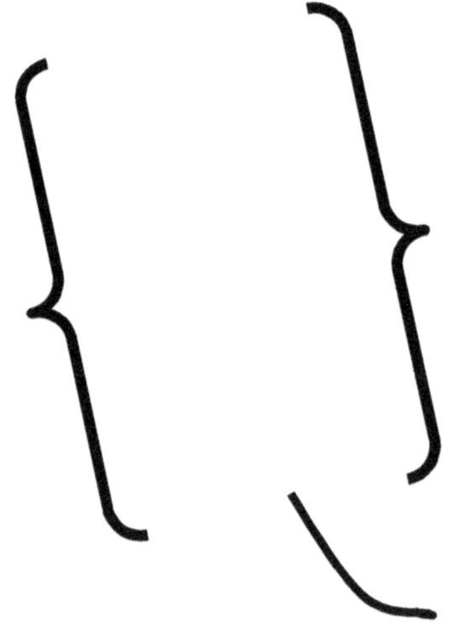

Rise! Rise! Rise!

I will go into the fiery air of Giver and Taker.

Rise! Rise! Rise!

I will go into the fiery air of Giver and Taker.

Rise! Rise! Rise!

I will go into the fiery air of Giver and Taker.

And down I will finally go to meet my fate for the last time…once more!

Until Once More Is No More And Into My Presence Of Unstained-Shelter.

Beneath My Folds Joy And Strength Welcome You Home! Come My Child! Home!

Exact

Written By David Darseli Santana

The

Exact

Is

Never

Exact.

In

This

World

The

Closest

Thing

To

Exact

Is

Proximity.

How then did we come to use this term?

In one dictionary we see it as an adjective, an adverb, a verb, and a noun.

As

An

Adjective

The

Term

Means

Precision.

Which in turn

Means

Definite.

Which in turn

Means…

"Having distinct limits; known positively; clearly defined."

Exact

Is

Never

Exact

For

The

Flow

Of

Creation

Is

Never

Fixed

Its points are on a continual flow of motion

Which

Is

Determined

Only at points

Of

Creation

Being

Set

Forth

For

Further

Progression

That

In

Turn

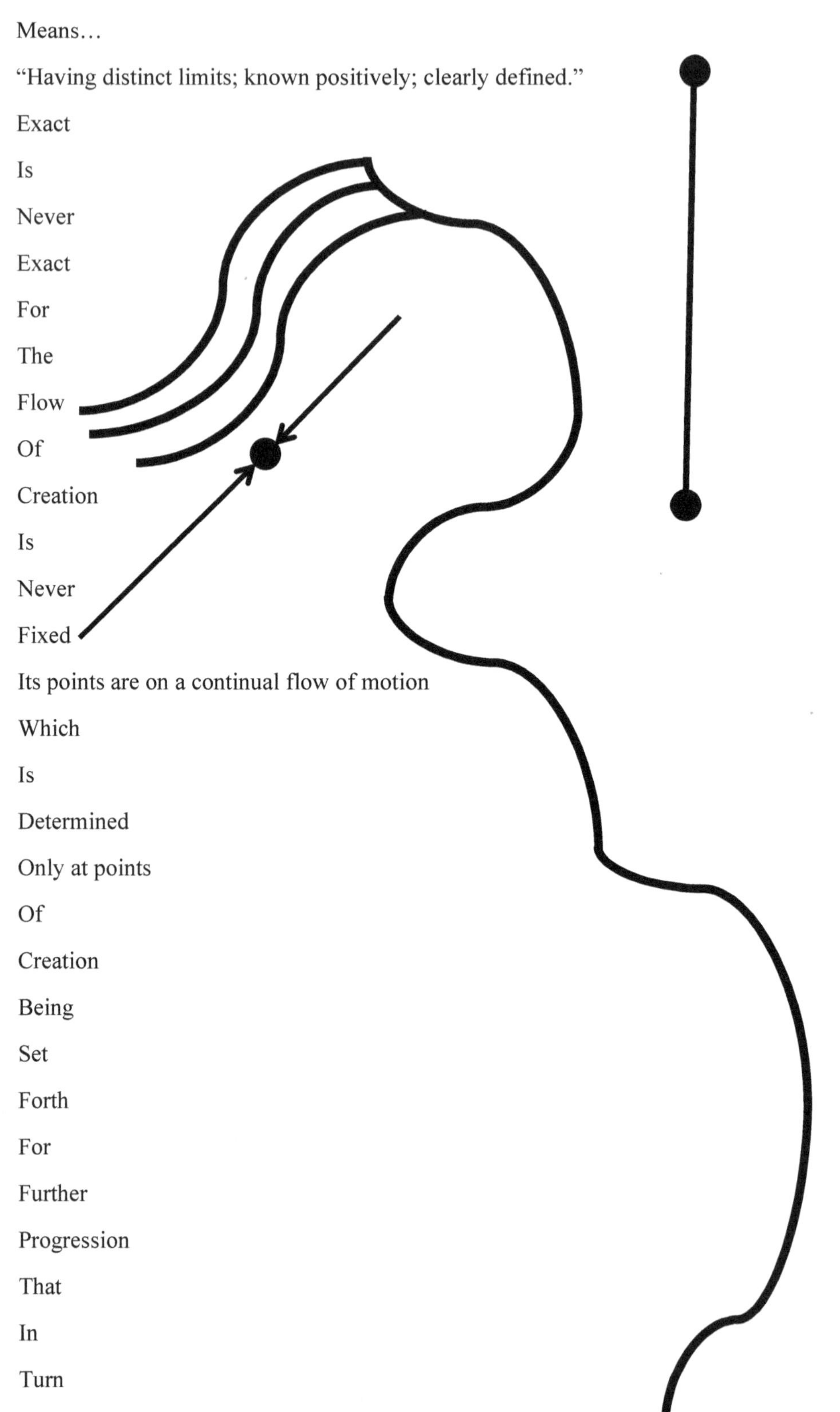

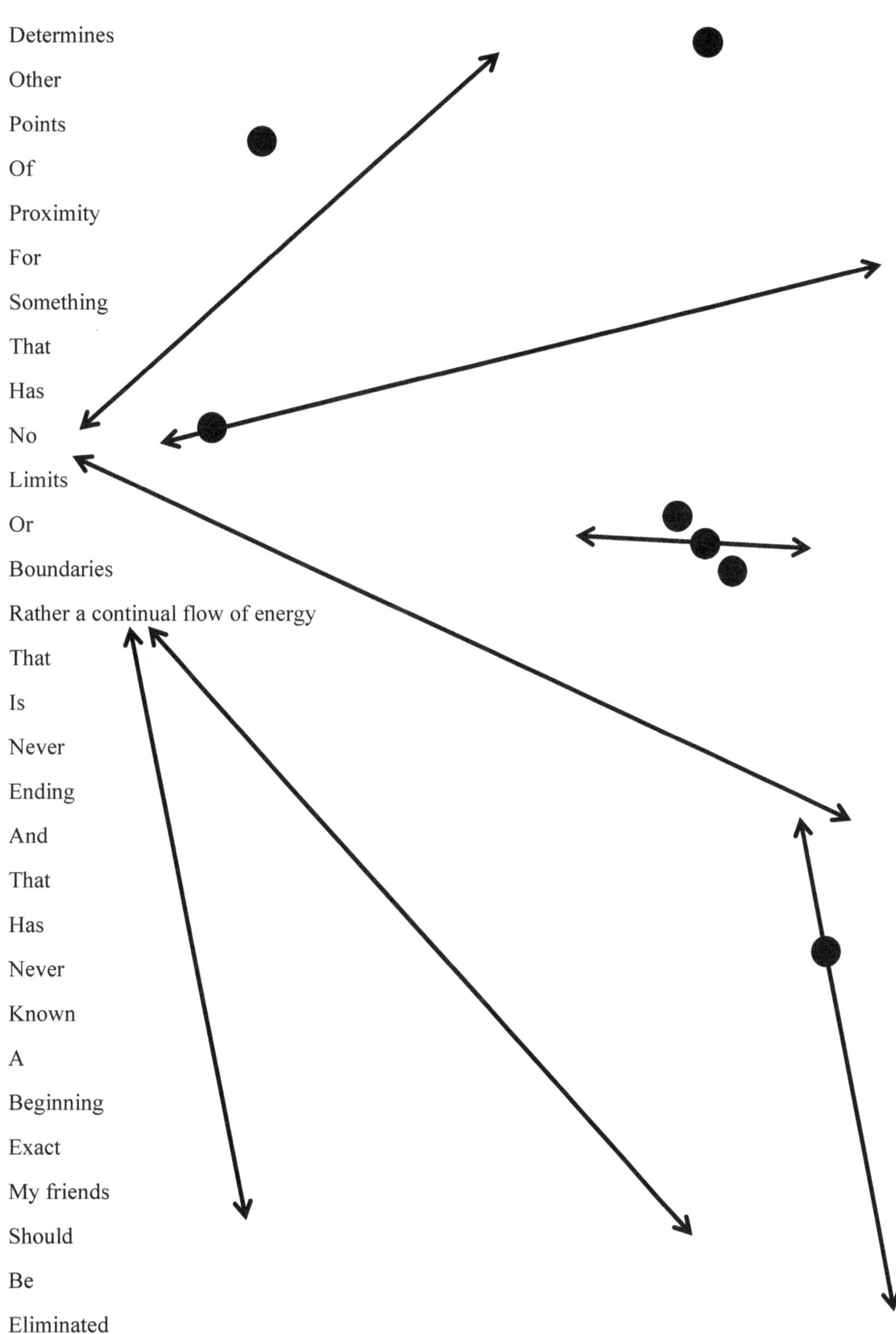

Determines
Other
Points
Of
Proximity
For
Something
That
Has
No
Limits
Or
Boundaries
Rather a continual flow of energy
That
Is
Never
Ending
And
That
Has
Never
Known
A
Beginning
Exact
My friends
Should
Be
Eliminated

From

Our

Vocabulary

For it distorts

Misguides

The

Reality

Of

What

We

Are

And

Of

What

Is

Around

Us

And

Of

What

Is

Good

In

This

World

Signed:

David

Darseli

Santana

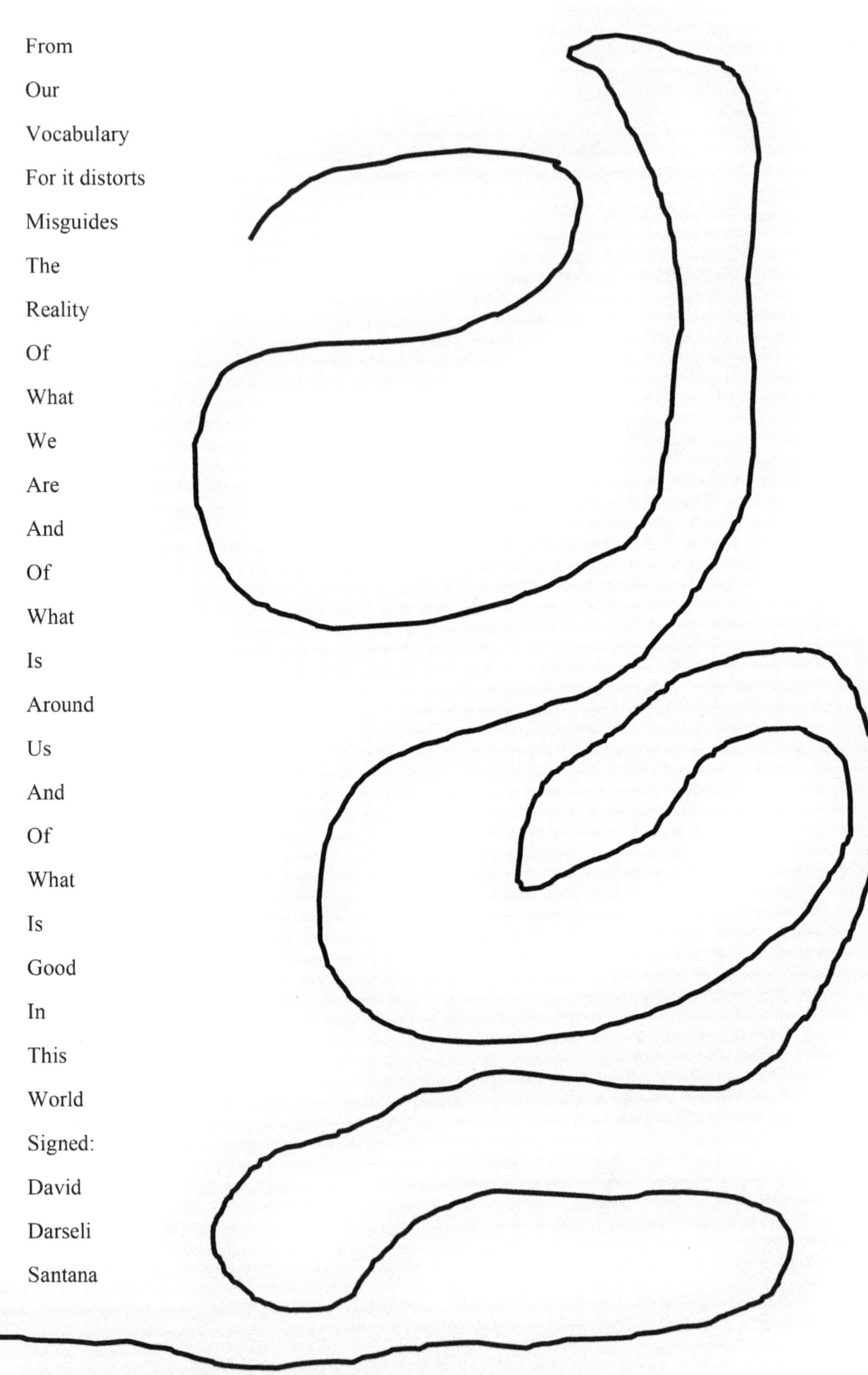

A Confused Mind at U.C.LA.
(1st Quarter! Thinking Out Loud On Paper)

Written By David Darseli Santana

Today I face a real challenge: To be calm and continue my academic curriculum. All my classes seem overwhelming and I'm afraid I don't fit well as a student of these subjects. I am frightened, pissed off, and confused.

I am frightened I suppose because I'm afraid I won't do well in these classes.

I am pissed off because I have to go through the agony of being afraid. I believe I have a complex--- feeling inferior to other students and I don't feel compatible.

I am confused because one moment I'm self-confident and the other I'm not. I really don't know which way I will sway; I don't feel in control.

I ask: what will make me be a winner? Will it be better not to think of my load and continue semi-aware of them? I believe this is my only alternative I can conceive and really act on.

How can I retain long lasting or permanent self-confidence and fire?!!!

One solution is to be on top of everything all the time. I rarely accomplish this.

Another solution is to feed my self self-confidence day by day or minute by minute! How will I do this? I don't know.

WAIT!

In Retrospect, everything is bullshit. I wish I had never fallen for the trap of a higher education. It was a waste of time when it came to true happiness. In fact, going to college ruined by relationships because college demanded so much that IT left ME with little or no time for self-development, family, friends, fun times, relax times!.

<u>My recommendation friend:</u> Learn through OTHER means at your own pace! And give higher education the BOOT!!! What I say is true. Save yourself the trouble, the danger! Truly, David "J"

Eternal

Written By David Darseli Santana

I do not start my thinking on the subject of today arbitrarily.

Rather, today I write some more.

Subtleness abides in my mind as I ponder what I see, feel, and hear.

Subtleness abides in me while the ravishness of the knowledge seeps within me.

Insanity many times I feel pokes and pierces within me without abide.

Abide is what ultimately keeps me from complete atrocity of emotions. Not to say I have not reached it, but simply that I am still here with you!

In this world we see a true testament of **our ignorance and foolishness**.

Yet, the main topic of organization here is that of bringing us to The Knowledge.: That we are nothing more than a being within a moldable passing physical; that we are occupying this body, although people may doubt it, the trueness of what we are to become and where we came from is hidden from us intentionally!

Become!

Shall we not stay focused on the eternal?

Or shall we just indulge in our **delusions**? NoNoDelusionsNO!!!

Ah!

But how tempting it is just to stay and not see further.

Ah!

But you may have decided not to see further.

 But the truth will CREEP UP on you like a thief catches one unawares!

You may also think that eternity is awaiting us.

But

In

Actuality…

Should I speak?

Should I speak in actuality or in metaphors or puns for you to see what you are?

Should I divulge the secrets which in fact are no secrets at all?

Listen my friend.

Shall I tell you what your heart desires or what your ears carelessly decide to take in?

Take in but for what cause and to what affect and effect?

We are eternal my friends. Period.

Our life in this world is but a phase in our continuity

A continuity that has no end and no beginning

That is, if you look beyond the physical features which lie…LIE!

Which LIE before you!

Before you!

Yes, there it is a beginning and an end.

…that is true **Only In This World** Run by Satan itself!

Yet it does not abide of what you are! There is Hope my friend!

Faith you must take into your mind!

What are you?

Listen As I Speak To You.

Listen carefully….¡cuidadosamente! soigneusement!

Perhaps. Perhaps. Perhaps. ..go to accuratamente mindset!

You will understand when the time of end and start assigned to you has passed! …go to sorgfältig mindset!

I shall again make this explicitly clear for you so that you may one day be free while you still abide in this prison-body assigned to you!

Here is the truth:

You Are Eternal. You Are Loved. You Are Welcomed Back Home! This World is NOT your home. We are Prisoners Here. There is a conspiracy to drain you of your energy! God wins! Extend Your hand and His Hand will extend to yours! **Believe Not Ambitions Of This World.** Rather: Believe in God and All that He is: Goodness, Compassion, Forgiving, Loving, Wanting you Back!

Come Take My Hand!

Beautiful Teen
(Memoir of a past!)

Written By David Darseli Santana

I look out and I see you.

You take a glance and we meet!

Beautiful Teen

Ready for life beyond home.

 I was just two years older

and knew

 I wanted to hold you!

Beautiful Teen

Ready for life beyond home

The spot light

The music

The glitter

In your eyes

slowed our vibrant start.

Beautiful Teen

Ready for life beyond home

Wanting to know

The Glamour

kept at a distance.

But now it is your turn to experience what you've only seen your mother do!

To prepare

to dress

in that beautiful gown of your dreams.

Beautiful Teen

Ready for life beyond home.

The sky is dark.

The lights of the night light up the sky.

You walk without a care in the world.

You talk without caring what you say.

I Just want to love you. I say!

You just want to dance!

I just want a steady love I say! (you are not ready for one).

Beautiful Teen

Ready for life beyond the home.

Beautiful Teen

Ready for life beyond the home.

Beautiful Teen

Ready for life beyond the home.

I understand you're not ready for love.

I   understand understand understand!

 Beautiful Teen

I love you!

¡Maldita Suerte!

Escrito Por David Darseli Santana

El tiempo pasa y todo sigue igual. **Maldita suerte me detiene en mi lugar. Todo por afuera se ve muy bien pero por dentro se está quebrando la fe que tanto proclaman en las iglesias.

*Todo control, amarrado estamos por la sociedad, la suciedad que maneja toda la libertad, el pensamiento, el dinero, la paz y tranquilidad

+Por las noches me quedo inquieto, no puedo dormir; pensando en las injusticias que rodean mis pasos. Soñando, no puedo soñar. Estamos en tanta mierda que no podemos subir la cabeza.

*Todo control, amarrado estamos por la sociedad, la suciedad que maneja toda la libertad, el pensamiento, el dinero, la paz y tranquilidad

xxx Corporaciones buscando maneras de hacer más dinero. No importa si el método es pisotear las manos, las cabezas de los empleados y las familias y los niños de bajos recursos.

++ ¿Qué es esto? ¿Qué pasa con el amor?

¿Qué pasa con la simpatía?

¿Qué pasa con el cariño?, ¿esta vida?

 **Maldita suerte me detiene en mi lugar. Todo por afuera se ve muy bien pero por dentro se está quebrando la fe que tanto proclaman en las iglesias.

*Todo control, amarrado estamos por la sociedad, la suciedad que maneja toda la libertad, el pensamiento, el dinero, la paz y tranquilidad

+Por las noches me quedo inquieto, no puedo dormir; pensando en las injusticias que rodean mis pasos. Soñando, no puedo soñar. Estamos en tanta mierda que no podemos subir la cabeza.

cabeza   cabeza   ¡cabeza!

++ ¿Qué es esto? ¿Qué pasa con el amor?

¿Qué pasa con la simpatía?

¿Qué pasa con el cariño?, ¿esta vida?

vida   vida   ¡vida!

¡Salguemos de la ignorancia y el control que nos maneja!

Comunidad Tiene La Clave Del Amor Verdadero.

Poder De Comunidad; no el poder de gobiernos. ¡Ancianos Levantencen!

El Amor De Cristo Y El Poder Del Padre Trae El Amor Verdadero Y Eterno.

Ravenoconda

Written by David Darseli Santana

Will you stay with me
I know that you see me
Riding in your eyes

What will it take for you
To give the gem
That resides in the
Deepest enticements
Leaves me in awe.

riding the lie, living the lie, let it end

I know that you love me
The truce will end in glory
It will bring Down all winds in the mist!

Dancing in glory and feeling the
Awe of the mystical lashes that bring me here

Ravenoconda. It will cease. It will decease

And out from the darkness a Gem will go out to carve

Carve and Etch Out A New World!

A New World For You For Me! For Us!

Ravenoconda. It will cease. It will decease

Glory At The Helm Of An Extinguished Deceit!

S o o t h

Written by David Darseli Santana

**Life comes
And takes you on a ride
Guaranteeing
That it will
Come to an end
Someday-yea.**

**Probable
Improbable is your
Destiny**

**Singing my
Lungs out I
I'm Hoping for the sooth.**

Prizes I've Gotten but I I need the sooth

**I wished upon a dream
it seems
To Mean to tell the tale that of sooths
That sooths
That never Gives in
But always
Radiate about
Running about
Running through my mind
My heart My soul My mind My heart My soul My life**

**Singing my
lungs out I
I'm Hoping for the sooth**

**Prizes I've Gotten but I
I need the sooth**

**I Wished upon a Dream it seems
To mean to tell the Tale of sooths
Sooths That never give in
But always Radiate about Running through my mind My heart!**

My soul My mind My soul My heart My life!

Singing my Lungs out

I I'm Hoping for the sooth.

Prizes I've Gotten but I I need the sooth

Ri sing
Ri sing
Clockworks
Yea.

When Life Doesn't Care

(my explicit relationship with God Father-referenced here)

Words and Music by David Darseli Santana a.k.a. Mystic Black

Searching for answers
Wanting to be with you again
Time and around
Spins for you
How easy it feels
To be with you
When life doesn't care
For the feeling I
Have for you
For you

Wouldn't it be nice
To be with you
In a world
With no faults

Where you could be you
Where I can be me
Where everything flows
To the truth
To the light
Oooh yea
To the truth
To the light

I
flow
to
you
to you
Flow
To
you

To you   Flow   To you

Longing For You

Words and Music by David Darseli Santana a.k.a.Mystic Black

Lumines[cense] skies
Fragile mind
I need you here
Here with me

The door
That is long
I love you
Stay here with me
While in this world
While in this maze

I must find a way
To you
Find a way
To you

Oh

It's been such a crowd
It's been such a wait
To be with you
To aaaaii

I love you
Show me the way

Thunder

Words and Music by David Darseli Santana a.k.a. Mystic Black

[Truth in fears]
[Truth in lies]
[Oooh Oooh Oooh]

I need you here
In this world of broken dreams
Surrounded by lying tongues
Manipulation breaks it all away
In your tender heart

Love and Lust reign
Broken hearts keep on breakin'
In this Roller Coaster [of death]
Of Lies and deceits
ooh no [man]

What will I do?

Open flesh, broken hearts go by
Seeking to be true to love
Let it lie

Watch it go by
Watch it go by
Watch it go by
Watch it die

white Covered Lies

Words and Music by David Darseli Santana a.k.a. Mystic Black

Come to me babe
More if you may
I don't need you
More than you do

Listen to the sky
What do you hear?

Everyday [you come by my way]
Scenes of the lost
Circumstance surmise
Don't you despise
[Don't you demise]
What you hear in me
Water runnin' high
Seeping to the brier
Of the other side

I want you now
To be open sky
In this yellow vice
In this yellow price

Of circumstance surmise
Giving it surprise
Don't you despise
The fruit of your 'mise

[Sing the bellow dry
Look at your demise
Subtle in the sky]

Yellow is vice
Subtle and dry
Whose hand is in the brier?
See the witches sigh
Yellow inside
Giving the lie

Don't you despise
Don't you demise

Hold the truth
Tear out the lie

Watch it go by
In Southern skies

Grip the Truth
Tear out the lie
Leave it behind
Leave it to die

Say the Word
Give up the lie
Let it lie
In Southern skies

Witches go by
Pouring the lie
Seeking your death
Seeking your 'mise

Yellow 'mise
White covered lies

Ooooh death
What a lie

Ooouuuuh
Aaaahaaa
Ooouuuu
Yeayeaa

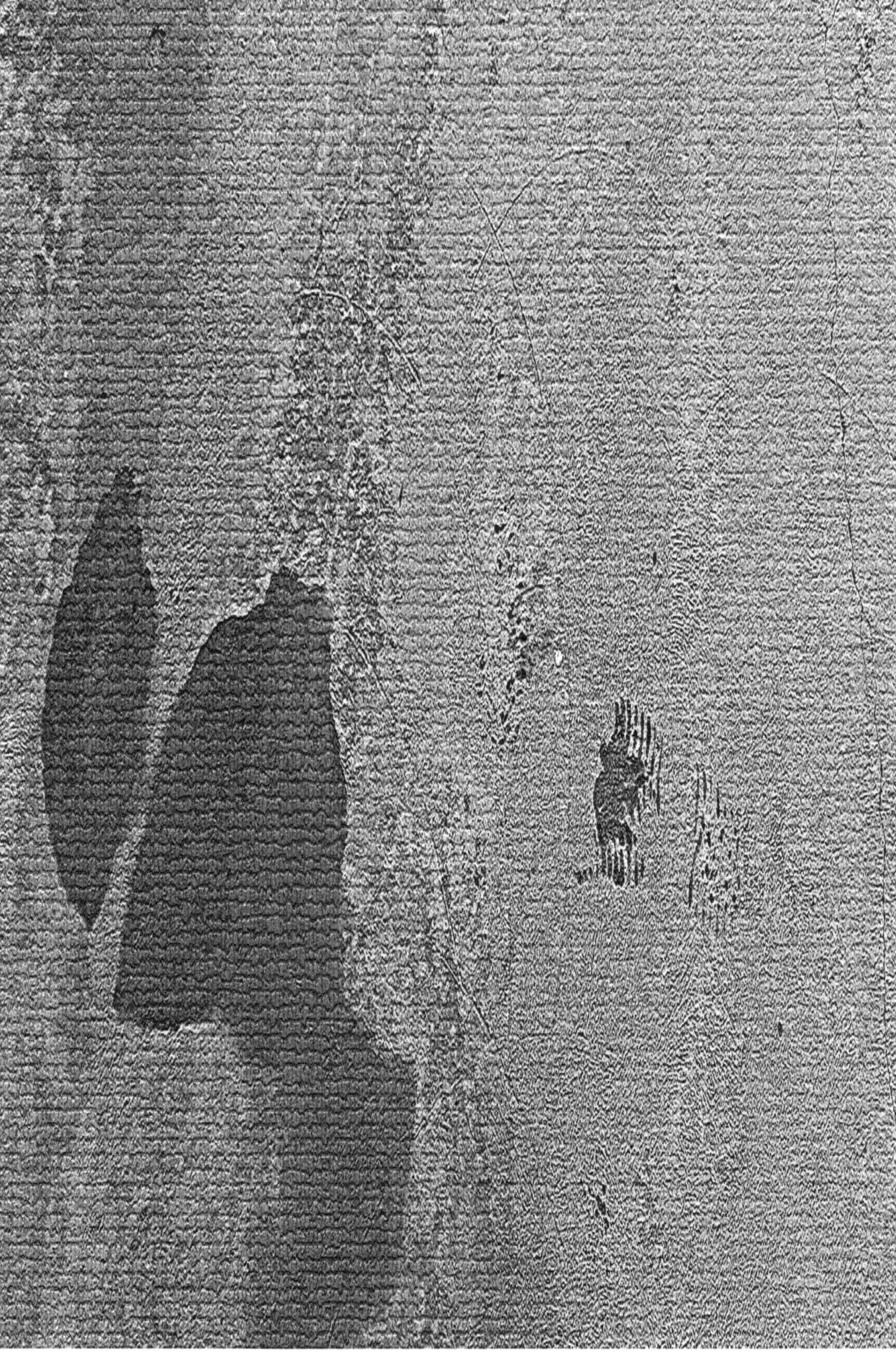

"MAY THE TRUTH BE SAID"

A Message

To My Fellow Spirit,

As we travel on this boat (whether by choice, condemnation, design, or will), one thing is certain, the truth of this existence is intentionally hidden from us. It seems that lies are everywhere: propagating a reality that is made up to distract us from the truth of who we really are.

What is practiced everywhere around us?: division. It is clear that that is the intent.... a mechanism that is as complex as this creation; a deceit that has multiple layers and languages...all serving the ultimate goal...to keep us blind.

Of course, there is one main purpose behind all this masquerading done by the media (print, television, movies, news), by historians, and by the actors (whether they know it or not, in being part of meeting the ultimate goal that is hidden); a will that is not our will; a will that seeks to consume our energy once we leave this prison body: the human body.

By now you may think me completely insane; considering everything I am proposing is in complete opposite of how you have been programmed to think; to act; to behave. The powers that be hold your programming chip...they write it and you buy it! We buy it. The secret messages are all around you: it only takes but a realization from you to pause and think and look and see!

My desire and my will is to free you; so that you may prepare yourself to be strong in spirit before the wrath that comes after the ceasement of your current confinement.

But the good news is the truth...the truth is: that regardless of their efforts for It, they will not succeed but be consumed by that which will end all Creation. For everything must return to the Source...be it in whole or in parts....but refined to its purity....bringing everything into harmony; and ending this division, this lie.

With all honesty,

David Darseli Santana
Friday, June 28, 2013
(10 years to bring you this message: 2023)

www.ingramcontent.com/pod-product-compliance
Lightning Source LLC
Chambersburg PA
CBHW040544170726
48295CB00012B/583